KU-187-250

'A gaudy, gorgeous celebration of the ever-connecting energies that run between the soul and the material, the self and the universe . . . the spirit of it is irresistible. It is Winterson's most vital work for years.' Ali Smith, *Scotsman*

'Jeanette Winterson is a writer of extraordinary gifts . . . she writes beautifully, truly and magically.' *Daily Telegraph*

'How beautiful. Writing of that calibre is almost four-dimensional.' *Financial Times*

'Phrase after phrase of perfect, thought-provoking poetry that plumbs the depths of truth and human frailty.' *Elle*

'A fascinating, shimmering fiction that provokes us into contemplating the nature of life – right down to its material composition – while at the same time feeding us with a portrait of love and tenderness that, for its un-expectedness, is doubly affecting.' *Scotland on Sunday*

'*Gut Symmetries* by Jeanette Winterson is an extraordinary work of Thought. This is a Philosophy of the love affair, an occult ritual between Physics and Imagination, the Animus and the Anima are out t'getcha. I love it.' *Don't Tell It*

GUT SYMMETRIES

JEANETTE WINTERSON is the author of five works of
fiction, a comic book, two screenplays and most recently a
collection of essays, *Art Objects*. She has received the
Whitbread Award, the John Llewellyn Rhys Prize, and the
E.M. Forster Award from the American Academy and
Institute of Arts and Letters.

Also by Jeanette Winterson

fiction
ORANGES ARE NOT THE ONLY FRUIT
THE PASSION
SEXING THE CHERRY
WRITTEN ON THE BODY
ART & LIES

comic book
BOATING FOR BEGINNERS

essays
ART OBJECTS

GUT SYMMETRIES

Jeanette Winterson

Granta Books
London

Granta Publications, 2/3 Hanover Yard, Noel Road,
London N1 8BE

First published in Great Britain by Granta Books 1997
This edition published by Granta Books 1998

'King's Mountain' by Muriel Rukeyser is reproduced
by kind permission of William L. Rukeyser from
A Muriel Rukeyser Reader, 1994, W. W. Norton, New York,
© William L. Rukeyser.

A CIP catalogue record for this book is available
from the British Library

1 3 5 7 9 10 8 6 4 2

Typeset in Bembo by M Rules
Printed and bound in Great Britain
by Mackays of Chatham PLC

For Peggy Reynolds
with love.

Special thanks to Frances Coady and her team at Granta Books. Thanks to Suzanne Gluck at ICM, Elisabeth Ruge at Berlin Verlag, Angela Leighton, Mrs Adrienne Reynolds, Henri Llewelyn Davies and my Jewish friends who taught me their love and mystery, especially Mona Howard.

Gratitude as ever to Don and Ruth Rendell who make things possible for me in so many ways.

CONTENTS

AUTHOR'S NOTE

Until the discovery of the planet Pluto in 1930, the sign of Scorpio was ruled by Mars. Since Paracelsus assumed Mars as his Ruler, I have used his system where he is concerned.

PROLOGUE

November 10 1493. Einsiedeln, Switzerland. Sun in Scorpio.

First there is the forest and inside the forest the clearing and inside the clearing the cabin and inside the cabin the mother and inside the mother the child and inside the child the mountain.

Paracelsus, physician, magician, alchemist, urge, demiurge, *deus et omnia* was born under the sign of the occult, ruled by Mars and driven by a mountain in his soul.

What do we know of him? That he was short and ugly. That he wore an oversize sword. That he wanted to be a hero and looked like a victim. There he was a bellicose, bellyaching, belching, belfry of a man with a pelvis like a beldam. So odd was the anatomy of this mis-bodied *bel esprit* that some hazarded his sex as female.

Man or manikin his genius brought him considerable reputation. If he had signed a pact with Mephistopheles, the Old

1

Deceiver did not reward him in the usual way. Paracelsus made enemies faster than he made friends, and he had a habit of re-beggaring himself whenever he was beginning to do well. Perhaps this was necessary for an alchemist who did not want to turn base metal into gold. Like his contemporary, Luther, Paracelsus wanted to change the whole world.

The sign of Scorpio takes as its symbols the scorpion and the eagle. If its higher nature is as lofty as its mountain haunts, its nether part is creviced and hostile. The poisoner and the scientist are one.

And both. Hired by the town of Basle to cure its epidemic of syphilis Paracelsus despatched as many as he re-hatched. The mediaevals were entrail-minded and Paracelsus often delivered his lectures over a scalpelled corpse. This was not the nineteenth-century model of diagnosis by pathology. It was, if it was anything, diagnosis by cosmology. Paracelsus was a student of Correspondences: 'As above, so below.' The zodiac in the sky is imprinted in the body. 'The galaxa goes through the belly.'

What is it that you contain?

The Dead. Time. Light patterns of millennia. The expanding universe opening in your gut. Are your twenty-three feet of intestines loaded with stars?

The Miracle of the One that the alchemists sought is not so very far from the infant theory of hyperspace, where all the seem-ing dislocations and separations of the atomic and sub-atomic worlds are unified into a co-operating whole. This is not possible in three spatial dimensions or even in four. Ten, at least, lure us out of what we know.

Star-dust that we are, will death lose its sting? Theoretically there will be no death, only an exchange of energy into what is likely to be another dimension.

The marriage of Heaven and Hell?

The old sceptics used to say that if Hell exists, where is it? What part of the Universe does it occupy? What are its coordinates? It had to be a latitudinal Hell, a longitudinal Hell. A Hell subject to tape measure and set square. The question 'Where is it' could not be answered satisfactorily.

Many tried. Traditionally, the afterlife lairs at the centre of the earth: Odysseus got in through a cave entrance in Persephone's Grove, while Virgil and Dante had only to look under the floorboards in Italy. In 1714, an Englishman, Tobias Swinden, published his *Enquiry into the Nature and Place of Hell* and concluded that Hell is on the Sun. In 1740, Whiston, Newton's successor as Professor of Mathematics at Cambridge, proved that Hell was somewhere in the regions of Saturn.

Such determined Hell-spotting may have had some sound science behind its normal devoutness and abnormal morbidity. Hell, we think, is hot. The waste heat generated by the endless stoking of sinful souls would be impressive. Heat gives us a clue. These days physicists scan beyond our solar system for evidence of heat emissions. The energy consumption of an advanced civilisation would be considerable and we should be able to detect its fall-out. As yet nothing. No spacemen, no Heaven, no Hell. But perhaps they have curled up on the Planck scale, in the six-dimension sister universe, smaller than small, bigger than big.

★

This is the theory.

In the beginning was a perfect ten-dimensional universe that cleaved into two. While ours, of three spatial dimensions and the oddity of time, expanded to fit our grossness, hers, of six dimensions wrapped itself away in tiny solitude.

This sister universe, contemplative, concealed, waits in our future as it has refused our past. It may be the symbol behind all our symbols. It may be the mandala of the East and the Grail of the West. The clouded mirror of lost beauty that human beings have stared into since we learned to become conscious of our own face.

Can anyone deny that we are haunted? What is it that crouches under the myths we have made? Always the physical presence of something split off.

Paradise: The Eden from which we have been forcibly removed.

The Twins: Missing self, other half, completeness again.

Male and Female: The uniting mystery of one flesh.

The Christ Motif: The Divine infills the human form and makes it whole.

Suppose the moment of Creation and our torn-off universe were recorded in the star-dust of our bodies? What is it that you contain? The atoms that you are were shook out of a star-burst ante-dating the Solar System.

We are the beginning. We are before time.

It may be that here in our provisional world of dualities

and oppositional pairs: black/white, good/evil, male/female, conscious/unconscious, Heaven/Hell, predatory/prey, we compulsively act out the drama of our beginning, when what was whole, halved, and seeks again its wholeness.

Have pity on this small blue planet searching through time and space.

Here follows a story of time, universe, love affair and New York. The Ship of Fools, a Jew, a diamond, a dream. A working-class boy, a baby, a river, the sub-atomic joke of unstable matter.

TIME: A concept arising from change experienced or observed. A quantity measured by the angle through which the sun turns on its axis.
A moment in which things happen.

UNIVERSE: All that is. The Cosmos.

LOVE AFFAIR: *Amour* honourable or dishonourable.

NEW YORK: Manhattan Island. Latitude 40:46N Longitude 73:59W.

SHIP OF FOOLS: A mediaeval conceit. Lunatics/saints sailing after that which cannot be found.

JEW: A person of Hebrew descent or religion. A chosen one. *See* Old Testament.

DIAMOND: Crystallised carbon. The hardest of all minerals. A magic stone.

DREAM: An image of truth.

WORKING-CLASS BOY: Drive disc of Capitalism. Girl or boy. An unexploded dream.

BABY: A beginning. An epiphany. A culet.

RIVER: *See* Einstein, Heraclitus, the Mersey, the Hudson, Time.

MATTER: A witticism. At sub-atomic level, that which has a tendency to exist.

THE FOOL

It began on a boat, like *The Tempest*, like *Moby Dick*, a finite enclosure of floating space, a model of the world in little. Here is a vas hermeticum, a sealed capsule on a rough sea. This is the alchemic vessel, resistant to change, constantly being transformed. This is us, vulnerable, insulated, entirely self-contained yet altogether at the mercy of the elements. The Ship of Fools is sailing tonight and all of us are aboard.

This is a true story. If it seems strange, ask yourself, 'What is not strange?' If it seems unlikely, ask yourself, 'What is likely?'

Any measurement must take into account the position of the observer. There is no such thing as measurement absolute, there is only measurement relative. Relative to what is an important part of the question.

This has been my difficulty. The difficulty with my life. Those well-built trig points, those physical determinants of parents, background, school, family, birth, marriage, death, love, work, are themselves as much in motion as I am. What should be stable, shifts. What I am told is solid, slips. The sensible strong ordinary world of fixity is a folklore. The earth is not flat. Geometry cedes to algebra. The Greeks were wrong.

Those Greeks, who too began in boats, are the root of Western science, a science that has taken 2,500 years to find its way back to the meaning of its premise. In the sixth century BC, the Milesians of Iona deeply concerned themselves with what they called 'physis', that is, nature, the nature of things; spirit, man, the observable world, the heavenly bodies.

By the fifth century, Heraclitus was teaching his doctrine of eternal Becoming, flux not fix, an identity of perpetual change, process not substance, the flow that made it impossible to step into the same river twice.

His rival, Parmenides, a man for whom nothing changed, taught instead the supremacy of godhead and the certainty of matter. Either things existed or they did not. Becoming was challenged by Being.

Since unalterable Being and perpetual Becoming could not be reconciled, the Greeks fashioned the ingenious compromise of dividing spirit and matter. Written along the clear line of demarcation was the new view of the Atomists that matter was made out of basic building blocks; passive intrinsically dead particles, moving in a void. Their movement was controlled by the individual spirit of man and the over-spirit of god.

This cosmic picture, so well-known to us that it has become axiomatic, was systematised and refined by Aristotle. Matter and

Mind, Matter and Form, were persuasively interpreted and later incorporated entire by developing Christianity. That science and the Church should be tied together until the Renaissance was made possible by the dualistic system of the mundane and the miraculous that suited the world-view of both interested parties.

The tenacity of the model should not be underestimated. Newton made it the basis for his Mechanics in the seventeenth century and rested his clockwork universe firmly in the principles of Euclid. Firming up Greek thought, it was Newton who realised concepts of absolute space and absolute time. Newton who regarded the Universe as three-dimensional, solid, massy, hard, made up of the motion of material points in space, a motion caused by their mutual attraction, that is, the force of gravity.

The mathematics he developed to explain his proposals were of such astounding success that no one thought to enquire behind them into the validity of the Newtonian world itself. His theories remained triumphant and unchallenged until 1905 when Albert Einstein published two papers; one, his 'Special Theory of Relativity', and the other, a look at the disturbing implications of electromagnetic radiation. These were the beginnings of quantum physics and the end of the mechanistic, deterministic, mind/matter of cosmic reality.

Forgive me if I digress. I cannot tell you who I am unless I tell you why I am. I cannot help you to take a measurement until we both know where we stand.

This is the difficulty. Now that physics is proving the intelligence of the universe what are we to do about the stupidity of humankind? I include myself. I know that the earth is not flat but my feet are. I know that space is curved but my brain has been cordoned by habit to grow in a straight line. What I call light is my own blend of darkness. What I call a view is my hand-painted *trompe-l'oeil*. I run after knowledge like a ferret down a ferret hole. My limitations, I call the boundaries of what can be known. I interpret the world by confusing other people's psychology with my own. I say I am open-minded but what I think is.

According to Darwin the evolutionist, man stood upright when he shed his saurian tail. What happened to it? Here it is, in my hand, like a motley joke of the *commedia dell'arte*. My fool's wand, my visible weakness, dropped off the back only to run round the front. I am civilised but my needs are not. What it is that lashes in the darkness?

What or who? I cannot name myself. The alchemists worked with a magic mirror, using reflection to guide them. The hall of mirrors set around me has been angled to distort. Is that me in the shop-glass? Is that me in the family photo? Is that me in the office window? Is that me in the silvered pages of a magazine? Is that me in the broken bottles on the street? Everywhere I go, reflection. Everywhere a caught image of who I am. In all of that who am I?

My suspicions were aroused when I was quite young. I could not find myself in the looking glasses offered. I could not define myself in relation to the shifting poles of certainty that seemed so reliable. What was the true nature of the world? What was the true nature of myself in it?

I could not immunise myself against the germ warfare of object and dream. There seemed to be no bridge between mind and matter, between myself and the world, no point of reference that was not a handy deception.

I tried to copy my parents, as monkeys do, but they were trying to copy me, looking to the child for the energy and hope they had long since lost.

I tried to copy other children but lacked their tough skin. I was a glove turned inside-out, softness showing. I was the visceral place between mouth and bowel, the region of digestion and rumination. No doubt it is my spleen that refuses to locate the seat of reason in the head. No doubt it is my natural acidity that fears the milkiness of the heart.

This story is a journey through the thinking gut.

It began on a boat.

The *QE2*. Southampton to New York and on to Los Angeles via the Panama Canal. A spring cruise of fun and fantasy where each day had been labelled with a mortician's care. There was an undertaker on board but his services are not usually required. For a few days, at least, the expensive antibodies of illusion and excess are sufficient to stall the effects of ageing and apathy, jolting even the most coffin-like into pink cheeked pleasure.

Pleasure = consumption.

After only six hours at sea my dauntless fellow travellers had begun to jowl their way through 2,455 lb of butter, 595 lb of frozen prawns, 865 gallons of ice cream, 26,500 tea bags, 995 lb of frozen fish, 135 jars of baby food, 170 bottles of vodka, 1,959 lb of lobster . . . the list is not endless but it is long. In a few days, these gut-defying deck chair adventurers will have vanished the lot in an orgy of Now You See It Now You Don't. I doubt whether our resident magician will perform such prodigious feats of disappearance. I said in my lecture this morning that the dining rooms of the *QE2* were proof positive of a fourth spatial dimension; there can be no ordinary human explanation for the daily loss of so much matter.

It is remarkable, at sea, how delicate appetites, special diets, macrobiotic tendencies, and Yin-Yang energy alignments fall victim one and all to the Dionysiac phrensy of champagne (1,160 bottles) and caviare (55 lb). The unworldly should remember that caviare is normally eaten by the ounce.

Inevitably it is not only the gastric juices that are stimulated by luxury and fresh air. What could be nicer than pre-prandial fellatio in a foreign tongue?

The Exotic, the Other, the orient of interest that floats at sea. Where else could anyone have access to a Thai chambermaid, a bored Countess, a fading rock star and a briny boy, all for the effort of a stroll on deck?

Here is a Faustian world of self-gratification. Set outside of time, it looks real, it tastes real, inevitably it vanishes. If that brings bitterness it also removes responsibility. Outside of time there is no responsibility.

HE: Are you married?

ME: No.

ME: Are you married?

HE: Yes.

There was a long pause.

HE: My wife and I live on different planets.

ME: Are you separated?

HE: We have our own bathrooms.

After my opening lecture on Paracelsus and the new physics, a balding man, bristling with energy, had bounded up to me and grasped my hand, hands, no matter how many I might have had, he would have grasped them all. He introduced himself as my companion lecturer for Cunard's spring cruise, theme, 'The World and Other Places'.

The world of physics has few places more prestigious than the Institute for Advanced Studies, Princeton, New Jersey. This man, Jove, was based there, working on a new model of the cosmos, dimensionality of hyperspace, ghost universes symmetrical with ours. He was the future.

I said 'You are the future.'

He said 'Does time wear a watch?'

Jove was lecturing on Time Travel. Every morning he had to explain to elderly gentlemen why they would not be able to regain their hairline by stepping into a time machine. No one was interested in Einstein's General Theory of Relativity and its impact on what we call time. Everyone wanted to know when they would be able to extend their lives indefinitely by living them backwards. Theoretically it is possible to slow down the effects of ageing by altering the rate of time. Travelling at speeds close to those of light (186,000 miles per second), time's flow trickles. If we break the light barrier, time seems to go backwards, that is, we need no longer move forwards.

'They want me to tell them how to find Reverse,' said Jove, 'when most of them have spent sixty years wondering how to shift out of Automatic into First.'

I did not believe in fate but it can be a useful excuse.

How strange that I should be working my passage to New York, bags in the hold, my body harbouring a new start.

How strange that I should have won two years of research funding at Princeton.

How strange that I would be seeing this man every day.

As the rest of the audience shuffled away to their favourite binary opposition, gin/tonic, a woman came forward and asked Jove, 'If we were to travel back in time would it be advisable to don the costume of that period before we set off or to buy it when we get there?'

What a fashion opportunity. While the physics fraternity are just beginning to wrestle with the implications of time travel, the travellers are worrying about what to wear. The world is ready for Ralph Lauren Mediaeval.

'I'll leave you ladies to discuss it,' said Jove.

'Wait,' I said. 'You are the one in the Armani,' and I walked away.

He caught up with me later, part furious, part beaten.

'You should meet my wife.'

'How will I know which bathroom to use?'

I said there was a love affair. In fact there are two. Male and female God created them and I fell in love with them both.

If you want to know how a mistress marriage works, ask a triangle. In Euclidean geometry the angles of a triangle add up to 180 degrees and parallel lines never meet. Everyone knows the score, and the women are held in tension, away from one another. The shape is beguiling and it could be understood as a new geometry of family life.

Unfortunately, Euclidean theorems work only if space is flat.

In curved space, the angles over-add themselves and parallel lines always meet.

His wife, his mistress, met.

Perhaps if this story had happened before 1856 I should not be telling it to you at all.

In the nineteenth century, most people knew their place, even if they did not know the mathematics that predicated it. In a strictly three-dimensional world, where the shortest distance between two points is a straight line, the comings and goings of sexual intrigue could be measured with a reassuring accuracy. On a flat sea the boat hardly rocks. What happens when the sea itself plunges away?

1856. A poor obscure tubercular German called Reimann delivered a lecture calculating that Euclid is valid only in terms of flat surfaces. If the surface were to turn out not to be flat then two thousand years of mathematical smugness might not be smiling.

Sixty years later, a poor obscure German called Einstein realised that light beams bend under gravity. Therefore, the shortest distance between two points is a curve.

If light travelled in a curved line it would mean that space itself is curved.

(Pitch of her body under me.)

'Alice?'

I could see him standing behind me. He wrapped himself rug-like round my shoulders. We made an elegant pair: dark/fair, older/younger, assured/uncertain. The mirror offered us a snapshot of our own desirability. He was gazing past me with some satisfaction.

I looked too, but what disturbed me was another face in the mirror and another room behind.

It began. Of course it did. Simple, solid, knowable, confined. A love affair. A commonality of life as dependable as life itself. We are what we know. We know what we are. We reflect our reality. Our reality reflects us. What would happen if the image smashed the glass?

'Ice?' Jove handed me my drink.

'How many more of them will ask me whether or not they should be refrigerated at death until science can defrost them into the warmth of perpetual youth?'

'What do you say?'

'What I should say is that if you go in like a turkey you will come out like a turkey.'

ME: What will you do with your old age?

HE: What I have done with my youth and middle age.

ME: Your work?

HE: *Purché porti la gonnella, Voi sapete quel che fa.* (He sang.)

ME: If she wears . . .? *La gonnella?*

HE: A petticoat.

ME: You know what he does.

HE: *Don Giovanni*. I'll take you to the Met. I'll take you everywhere.

That's how it was/is. The story falters. The firm surface gives way. Nine months ago I was on this boat sailing towards my future. Nine months later and I am balanced on it as precariously as if it were a raft. On this raft I am trying to untangle my past. My past/our past. Jove had a wife. I was in love with them both.

That's how it is/was. Jove and his wife have disappeared. He crying in salt waterfalls, she scattering her tears like gunshot. I should have been with them.

Why was I not?

Here I am, all aboard the eternal triangle reduced to a not quite straight line.

Here I am, man overboard, woman too. They are gone but there are no bodies.

I am still here but there is no feeling. I cry lead.

If there was a body perhaps I could feel. He would say if I could feel there would be a body. Energy precedes matter.

She would say 'Until you are ready to love there is no one to love.' Would say/did say, caught in the curve of her own light.

Is that her breast under me? Sphere of the thinking universe, wilful plunge of the sea?

Stabs of time torment me. What use is it to go back over those high rocks that resist erosion? My life seems to be made up of dark matter that pushes out of easy unconsciousness so that I stop and stumble, unable to pass smoothly as other people do. I should like to ramble over the past as though it were a favourite walk. Walk with me, memory to memory, the shared path, the mutual view.

Walk with me. The past lies in wait. It is not behind. It seems to be in front. How else could it trip me as I start to run?

Past. Present. Future. The rational divisions of the rational life. And always underneath, in dreams, in recollections, in the moment of hesitation on a busy street, the hunch that life is not rational, not divided. That the mirrored compartments could break.

I chose to study time in order to outwit it.

When I was ten I heard my headmaster tell my father, 'She'll never be top drawer.'

I looked at the pockets of their tweed coats, their knitted pullovers and knitted ties. I looked at their tawny jaws, their bottled eyes. I felt myself caught between two metal plates, crushing me. The pressure on my head was intense. I wanted to say 'Wait' but I was so low down that they could not possibly hear me. I lived in a world below their belts, not an adult not a child, smaller than small at the indeterminate age. The plates ground together and my father started to talk about the cricket.

We got home, my father and I, self-made man, poor boy made good, and while he poured himself a sherry, I went into my parents' room where they kept their chest of drawers.

There were two top drawers. My mother's held her jewellery and scent. My father's stored his handkerchiefs. His hobby was magic tricks.

When children learn to count they naturally add and multiply. Subtraction and division are harder to teach them, perhaps because reducing the world is an adult skill. I had long believed, and still did, that my father had at least two hundred handkerchiefs and that he had handkerchiefs as kings have treasure. Silk, spotted, plain, embroidered, cotton, paisley, patterned, striped, linen, raw, spun, dyed, lace like a periwig for his evening clothes. When he put one in his top pocket he sometimes gave it rabbit ears.

'Alice?'

And I followed him through corridors of make-believe and love.

Right at the back of the drawer was his gold watch; a full hunter that chimed every fifteen minutes. Essential for a man whose time was measured in quarter hours.

Is this what I would not be? Solid, reliable, valuable, conspicuous, extravagant, rare?

I scattered the handkerchiefs like soft jewels. Is this what I would not be? Fancy, impudent, useful, beautiful, multiple, various, witty, gay?

In what was left of the afternoon light I opened the lower drawers.

Underwear, talcum powder, balled up socks.

'Do you have to work so hard?' said my father, when I was anorexic and hollow eyed.

I got a scholarship to Cambridge to read physics and I started eating again. Of sleep I remained suspicious.

When I sleep I dream and when I dream I fall back into my fears. The gold watch is there, ticking time away, and I have often tried to climb inside it and jam the mechanism with my body. If I succeed, I go to sleep within my sleep, only to wake up violently because the watch is no longer ticking but I am.

I told this dream to my father who advised me to slow down. It was not necessary to win every prize for physics in the University.

There was a small mirror in my room. When I looked into it I did not see Alice, I saw underwear, talcum powder, balled up socks.

I know that my father feared for me a lonely old age and a lonely young one too. He did not say so, but the words behind the words told me that he would rather have launched me into a good marriage than watch me row against the tide at my own work. It remains that a woman with an incomplete emotional life has herself to blame, while a man with no time for his heart just needs a wife.

When I went up to Cambridge, my mother said to me, 'Alice, when you are at dinner with a man never look at your watch.'

Like many women of her generation she expected to let time run its course through her without attempting to alter it. Her timepiece was my father, and it was by his movement that she regulated her life. She liked his steady ticking, although she once admitted to me that he used to make her heart beat faster, in days when the sun on the sun-dial was a game.

They had come in from the garden, got married, settled down, and my father seemed not to mind the demands of his pocket watch. My mother never learned to be punctual and always has been vague about any appointment not directly connected to my father. She had a habit of taking my sisters and I to the dentist on the wrong day of the wrong week, and once, a year late. She had turned up a visit card in a coat pocket and marched us off to refill our filled molars. The dentist took it well. He said to my father, 'Women are like that.'

When my mother began any sentence with 'When you get older' I thought I would perish in despair. I knew that she never remembered to wind the clock and that I would stay the same age forever. Only with my father could there be a chance to grow up.

All children stumble over what Einstein discovered; that Time is relative. In mother-time the days had a chthonic quality, we ate, slept, drew, played, world without end, waiting without knowing we were waiting for my father to come home and snap his fingers and whisk us into the golden hour. We became aware, though I can't say how, that he was giving us four whole quarters of an hour. Perhaps that is when I began to study the vexed relationship of one minute to the next.

After we had been put to bed, my mother got an hour too, and I was glad that she and not we had to share her hour with the dinner. Then my father went into his study and the house was dark.

March 14 1879. Ulm. Germany. Sun in Pisces.

A man slow of speech and gentle of person. What patterns do the numbers make breaking and beginning in the waters of his spirit? He floats in numbers. Now he rests on a nine, now he swims hard against a seven, numbers iridescent, open mouthed, feeding off him as he feeds on them.

The numbers come when called. From the strange seas of the galaxy the numbers shoal to him. He knows the first words of Creation, and nearly sees, but not, the number that hides beneath. He hears the Word and tries to write the number but not all numbers are his.

The untamedness of numbers is in their order, resolving upwards into a speculated beauty. Too close and language fails. He believes that Number and Word are one and he speaks in numbers and words, trying to remake in his own body the unity he apprehends.

Einstein: the most famous scientist in the world. Everyone

knows about $E = MC^2$. Not everyone knows that: 'If a body falls freely it will not feel its own weight.'

The implications of this stretch beyond the theory of gravity they maintain.

I know I am a fool, trying to make connections out of scraps but how else is there to proceed? The fragmentariness of life makes coherence suspect but to babble is a different kind of treachery. Perhaps it is a vanity. Am I vain enough to assume you will understand me? No. So I go on puzzling over new joints for words, hoping that this time, one piece will slide smooth against the next.

Walk with me. Hand in hand through the nightmare of narrative, the neat sentences secret-nailed over meaning. Meaning mewed up like an anchorite, its vision in broken pieces behind the wall. And if we pull away the panelling, then what? Without the surface, what hope of contact, of conversation? How will I come to read the rawness inside?

The story of my day, the story of my life, the story of how we met, of what happened before we met. And every story I begin to tell talks across a story I cannot tell. And if I were not telling this story to you but to someone else, would it be the same story?

Walk with me, hand in hand through the neon and styrofoam. Walk the razor blades and the broken hearts. Walk the fortune and the fortune hunted. Walk the chop suey bars and the tract of stars.

I know I am a fool, hoping dirt and glory are both a kind of luminous paint; the humiliations and exaltations that light us up. I see like a bug, everything too large, the pressure of infinity hammering at my head. But how else to live, vertical that I am, pressed down and pressing up simultaneously? I cannot assume you will understand me. It is just as likely that as I invent what I want to say, you will invent what you want to hear. Some story we must have. Stray words on crumpled paper. A weak signal into the outer space of each other.

The probability of separate worlds meeting is very small. The lure of it is immense. We send starships. We fall in love.

Walk with me. On the night that Jove and I first slept together I left him half covered in the vulnerability of a strange bed and walked from Central Park down to the Battery. I don't own my emotions unless I can think about them. I am not afraid of feeling but I am afraid of feeling unthinkingly. I don't want to drown. My head is my heart's lifebelt.

I ignored the Stop-Go of the endless intersection traffic lights and took my chance across the quieted roads. Not night, not day, the city was suspended, its cries and shouts fainter now, its roar a rumble, like something far off. In the centre of it I felt like a creature on the edge. This is a city of edges, grand sharp, precipitous, unsafe. It is a city of corners not curves. Always a choice has to be made; which way now? A city of questions, mouthy and insolent, a built Sphinx to riddle at the old world.

I learned to feel comfortable in New York the way a fakir learns to feel comfortable on a bed of nails; enjoy it. Beauty and pain are not separate. That is so clear here. It is a crucible city, an alchemical vessel where dirt and glory do effect transformation. No one who succumbs to this city remains as they were. Its indifference is its possibility. Here you can be anything.

If you can. I was quite aware that much of what gets thrown into an alchemical jar is destroyed. Self-destroyed. The alchemical process breaks down substances according to their own laws. If there is anything vital, it will be distilled. If not . . .

Undeceive yourself Alice, a great part of you is trash.

True, but my hope lies in the rest.

I walked quickly, purposefully, wearing Jove's leather jacket. I wanted clothes about me because I felt I had been bone stripped. The solid knowable shape had gone. My flesh was there, part pleasure, part sore, and the antennae of my nervous system still processing the facts of a second body. The body is its own biosphere, air entering cautiously through an elaborate filter, food attacked by hostile acids. Nothing from outside is given a long-stay visa. Oxygen is expelled as carbon, even champagne and *foie gras* are pummelled into turds and piss. The body is efficient but not polite. It uses and discards. Enter a second body and there is some confusion. In or out? Which is it?

The curious fact of love is that it overrides the body's rubber-sealed selfishness. Sex and procreation easily fit in with the body's plans for Empire; it wants to extend its territory, needs to reproduce itself. It resists invasion. Love the invader compromises the self's autonomy. Love the rescuer is the hand held out across the uncrossable sea.

Trust it? Perhaps. It may be the right hand or something more sinister. My body is unconvinced, my mind would like to throw down the keys. I am of the generation brought up on romance. Where is the one for me?

Biologically there are thousands of ones for me. If I want to rut I can rut. I should be wary of ties that are chains and hands that are handcuffs. What should lead me out is very likely to wall me in. The bitterness of love is twin of its hope.

Walk with me. What kind of a woman goes to bed with another woman's husband? Answer: a worm? That might explain my invertebrate state. Boneless woman; heart breast and thighs, not the kind of woman I thought I was. If I am so ignorant of my own self, how can I claim knowledge of another human being?

My body still damp with him I am afraid.

'"Even the hairs of your head are numbered"' isn't that what God said?' Jove was lying on his back smiling at me. He rubbed his temples and pulled a face. 'In my case God need only count to twenty.'

Then he was serious, which he hardly ever seemed to be and he took hold of the weight of my hair. 'This is the mathematics of God.'

Later, admiring his own erection, he said, 'This is the physics of God.'

Both statements should be read carefully because Jove did not believe in God.

At the Battery I leaned on the rail and looked out at the water. There was a fog coming in and the lights of a tug blinking its coded message. The darkness and the water did not feel like a threat. Darkness-water felt like a response to the fluid place that had become my heart. As a scientist I try to work towards certainties. As a human being I seem to be moving away from them. If I needed any proof of the provisional nature of what is called the world I was beginning to find it. Of what could I be sure? Absolutely sure?

And yet I tended towards him as light to a bright object.

I realise that is an optical illusion.

I started to walk back, away from the water, away from the dark. I would have to go back into the day just beginning.

Love affair: *amour* honourable or dishonourable. Jove had a wife.

THE TOWER

My husband has started an affair. *Cherchez la femme.* Where is she?

Ransack the bedroom. The master bedroom well named. In a rip of pillow and sheet I shall tear her stigmata off the mattress. Is that her imprint, faint but discernible? My radioactive hands will sense her. Whatever bits of hair and flesh she has left behind I will find and crucible her.

Give me a pot and let me turn cannibal. I will feast on her with greater delight than he. If she is his titbit then I will gourmet her. Come here and discover what it is to be spiced, racked and savoured. I will eat her slowly to make her last longer. Whatever he has done I will do. Did he eat her? Then so will I. And spit her out.

I am not seeking revenge.

I am not a vengeful woman.

I must proceed reasonably.

Where is the screwdriver? I will have every hinge off every door. There will be no privacy in the bathroom. No place to read a billet-doux with one hand. Let him shave in front of me, shit in front of me, talcum powder his armpits under my stare. I will count the hairs on his razor and the rings around his tub. I will fact-find him as though he were a rare breed of insect.

I will do all this sanely.

Give me a drill. I will bore holes in his shoes and spy on him as he walks. Eyes beneath the pavement will be watching him. While he sleeps I will trepan the back of his head and with my fingers pull out his dream of her.

I shall of course be quiet.

Where is the chalk? I shall mark out a new Berlin Wall: two feet each in the hallway, his study he can keep, and the side of the drawing room that is furthest from the window. I will give him one lighted ring of the gas oven and the kitchen cold tap. Let him eat cake. I will mark the doorways as did the Jews on Passover and pray that the Angel of Death takes the male first born. Him.

The sex bed the love bed the afternoon and night bed where I held him he held her bed the ripe rotting sly bed. Where is the saw?

First sever the headboard. Second, disembowel the mattress. Third, gut the springs. Fourth, amputate the footboard. Fifth, neatly arrange the halves at either side of the room, one dazed blanket each.

Blankets? Blankets? What has he to do with blankets? Warm enough in borrowed arms. His secret heat.

At least I am still calm.

Her address. He must keep it somewhere.

I entered his study and began to go through his papers. What a
pretty avalanche of white. I began to think of last year when we
went skiing together and made love against the dunes of snow.

Look away. Who wants to salt themselves into a Lot's Wife of
memory?

Above all, now, do not give way to pain.

My hands shook and the papers under them and the study under
there and the stacked up lives below shook and the newsboy on
the news corner grabbed his news sheets and felt a second's agony
and did not know.

Where was she? Under the carpet? Pressed between the glass
and window frame? I was breathing her. Her dust, her molecules,
the air was fat with her, the droppings and gatherings of a living
body.

Purge the place, purge it.

I opened the windows of his study and conducted an experiment in gravity. If I drop a CD player and a lap top out of the same
window at the same time which one will hit the ground first?

Let the words fall with them. Hate. Anger. Pain. I have been
told that words are cheap. Words are light things that change nothing. Shuttlecock words raqueted between us. Nothing real only
skill in the play.

Why did the rubber and feather words not fall? Why did they
stick to my fingers? Photo frames and files I discus-hurled, watching them hold the air for a second before they dropped. I felt
Olympic. I was champion of the world.

I hurled and hurled and finally stood alone in the Buddha calm of his empty room. Breathe in. Breathe out.

My fingers were sticky. Hate. Anger. Pain. The words would not fall. I was bleeding words. I went into the bathroom to try to wash them away but when I drew back my hand from the clear cold water, the words welled up again, red and liquid, danger words, broken words, the cracked vessel of my love for him.

It was then that I began to cry. I knelt down, my head against the basin, filling it up like an offering with no one to whom I could offer it. A salty sea and no boat on it.

Blood and tears and crumbled words and words not fit for human use. Without love what does humanness mean?

YOU: Of course I love you.

ME: And someone else.

YOU: Sex . . .

ME: You talk as if it were an incurable disease.

YOU: Perhaps it is an incurable disease.

ME: I am the one who is suffering.

YOU: My feelings for you have never changed.

ME: How can you keep alive what is caught in its own death?

YOU: Words, words.

ME: Would you prefer I spoke in numbers? How many

times have you slept with her? How many months have you been seeing her? How old is she? What are her measurements? Does she reach orgasm quickly?

YOU: Stop it.

ME: Or not at all?

YOU: Calm down.

ME: Wife as walking Valium.

YOU: Look at this place . . .

ME: All my own work.

YOU: So I see.

ME: But you don't understand.

YOU: Men and women are different.

ME: You think I don't desire other men?

YOU: Who?

ME: Who, who, for a theoretical physicist you have a solid concrete brain. I desire other men. I don't sleep with them because I love you.

YOU: You should have been born a Catholic.

ME: For comfort?

YOU: For ambition. You might have been the first woman Pope.

ME: Cruel man.

YOU: Sorry. Just a joke.

ME: My husband the bedroom humorist.

YOU: Let me go into my study for a while. I have to think.

ME: Take a chair.

He frowned at me as though I were an inelegant equation; necessary but cumbersome, a bore to manipulate. I was no longer his living beauty of physical laws. No doubt he was telling her about the poetry of numbers. I looked in the mirror. Was that my face? I was gargoyled with grief. A stretched taunted thing. A waterspout of misery. He had poured his indifference down on me and I had let it out as dirty water. He thought I was the dirty water not himself.

Is it crazy to act crazy in a crazy situation? It has logic. It may even have dignity if dignity is what hallmarks the human spirit and preserves it.

I was not going to sink for him.

There was a noise from his study like a car that wouldn't start. A mix of roar and whine.

YOU: What have you done?

ME: I have thrown all of your things out of the window.

YOU: Why?

ME: To make me feel better.

YOU: You could have killed someone.

ME: I could have killed you.

YOU: This isn't making sense.

ME: There is no sense to what you have done. You didn't think about me when you were touching her. You threw me out of the window.

YOU: You jumped.

ME: What?

YOU: You have lived in your own world for years.

ME: You mean I haven't lived entirely in yours.

YOU: I don't expect that. I just expect . . .

ME: A little love and understanding.

YOU: Yes. Love and understanding.

ME: Then go and find it.

YOU: I'd better pack a bag.

He went into the exploded bedroom and returned with half a suitcase.

'What do you expect me to do with this?'

'Put it on your head.'

He flung it down and walked back through the doorway. Then he hesitated.

'What happened to the door?'

'It had an affair and left home.'

About half an hour later he came past me wearing three pairs of trousers, six sweaters, at least two shirts, his sports gear tied round his waist. In his arms he carried a bundle of assorted shoes and clothes.

'This is ridiculous.'

'Yes you are.'

I let him out of the one remaining door. He was going down the stairs when he seemed to remember something, or maybe something remembered him. He looked back at me as puddles of dirty water spilled round my feet.

'How did you find out?'

'She wrote to me.'

The morning mail. The sunny eight o'clock excrement of unasked for chances of a lifetime and unpaid bills. Buy a vibrating massage towel and win a trip to Iceland. Pay the electric company or spend the rest of your life in the dark. That morning I got a free gift of shampoo and an invitation to an introductory lecture on Transcendental dieting. Then there was a letter addressed to me. The handwriting was educated. The envelope was thick and square. I had no idea who it could be. I get a lot of letters. People like to write to writers. Now that poetry is fashionable again I have what might be called a following. I also have what might be called a leadering; the ones who write to tell me how to do it better. I thought the letter might be one of those.

I opened it. It was from a woman called Alice who said she was having an affair with my husband.

Cling. Pain upwards. Pain downwards. What corner of my insect world does pain not possess? The walls are smeared with it, sticky, slightly sweet. Pain is as total as a lover. I thought of those eighteenth-century engravings, German, where Death in his hood courts living flesh. This death is as obscene. The pictures in my head are sex and sex. I have become my own pornographer. His body. Her body. My body. Unseparated, twisting, dark. The grinning collusion of skulls boned in lust. The silent gravity-gone somersault of she on he on she. There we are, the infernal triangle, turning in the lubricious air, breasts, cock, cunt, oversized inflated parachutes of skin. I know we are falling, all three, but the ground is still a long way off. Until we grab each other like sky-divers. He was me I was him are we her? To vow yourself to someone else is to open a wound. From it blood flows freely, life of you to them. We call it blood brothers. We call it the dying Christ. The Fisher King's wound becomes him and will not heal. The vow of me to you and you to me is a red vulnerability on a grey shuttered world. We risk ourselves for each other, take the impossible step. Here is the knife that kills me in your hand. To prove it I let the blood myself. Monstrous, primitive, grand, divine, the one true extravagant gesture. The only thing I can claim to own is myself, and look, I shall give it to you, a ceremony of innocence made knowing in blood.

Don't say it was not so. We transfused each other. Now you want me to bleed to death so that no one can tell what wound it was we shared. It is not so simple. Vows can be broken; usually they are, but the wound tunnels deeper into the body one day to recur.

The Tower. Card XV of the Tarot deck. Two figures in identical dress explode from a shattered fortress.

Brick 1   Happiness. I love him he loves me.

Brick 2   Approval. I love him he loves me.

Brick 3   Security. I love him he loves me.

Brick 4   Time. I love him he loves me.

Brick 5   Complacency. I love him he loves me.

Brick 6   Indifference. I love him he loves me.

Brick 7   Apartness. I love me he loves him.

Brick 8   Refusal. I love him.

Brick 9   Lies. He loves me.

Brick 10   Danger. Love? Love?

Brick 11   One straw. One camel. Two backs.

The Tower. The safe walls are falling child.

I think back to Nimrod, the mighty hunter of Genesis, who built the Tower of Babel that God destroyed. Babel. Even when ruined, a man could walk for three days and still be in its shadow. What did I build that has called down such wrath?

I prefer to think of wrath on the outside and me on the inside. If I am a victim I cannot be the victimiser. The world is on my side here; rich and poor, sinner and saint, good man bad man, the murderer and the dead. I built a tower. I lived in it. Now it has been struck down. Did the lightning come like an indifferent god or did I draw it?

Don't imagine I torture myself with yesterday's washing up. A woman who slaves for a man does not have a marriage; she has a master. I don't want him at any price but I thought we had negotiated the price. Why did he go back to the market place looking for something cheaper?

When I lay down after reading the letter I could not speak or cry. My mind tried to force breathing pools under the dirty water. I seemed to find a bubble of air, and for a moment I could think clearly, then the waters closed again and I was back in the pain. Back in the sex. A stilted portfolio of anatomical drawings, genital insults pushed into my mouth and hair. Wherever I tried to rest my eyes, I saw the two of them making love. They were gessoed onto the walls and varnished into the floor. The chairs and tables that had belonged to my father were an Ottoman decoupage of delicate limbs and flaming breasts. Their arms, their legs, her belly against his, here in my house, like dry rot. I crawled into the kitchen away from the horror and opened my eyes. The fridge rubbed itself against me. The floor tiles were hot. As I clung to the door it clung back. I wiped my face with a dishcloth and smelled their sex.

To betray with a kiss. The reek of Judas. I took the brush to clean my teeth and thought of his mouth. Kiss of life, kiss of death. Come kiss me so that I can read your lips, deceptions scripted and waiting to be staged. His lying heart is in his mouth. When I kissed him this morning I tasted his fear.

HE: What's the matter with you?

ME: Nothing.

Nothing slowly clotting my arteries. Nothing slowly numbing my soul. Caught by nothing, saying nothing, nothingness becomes me. When I am nothing they will say, surprised, in the way that they are forever surprised, 'But there was nothing the matter with her.'

Nothing. Ashes to ashes, dust to dust, love to love.

When I was a child I imagined love as a glass well. I could lean over and dabble my hands in it and come up shining. It was not a current or a torrent, but it was deep and at its bottom, flowing. I knew it was flowing by the noise of the water over the subterranean pebbles. Were there ships in there and ports that depended on it, and harbours where people naturally built their settlements? I saw the world beneath the water only by reflection. To enter it would have meant climbing into the well and letting myself drop away. My mother cautioned me against swimming.

Day by day I returned to the edge, watching what I could, dabbling my hands. Later, when I was grown up, I met a man carrying two buckets, who plunged them into the pellucid waters, took one for himself and gave one to me. I had never held so much water. Never found any container that could. I lost interest in the well, I had my bucket.

Other people envied Jove and me. We were clean, wholesome, sexy, together. We displayed our marriage like a trophy and we did think that we had won it well. We polished the trophy but forgot to polish ourselves. As it shone brighter we dimmed. Did it matter if we were a little dusty, a little worn?

Our marriage became a thing apart; that is, a thing apart from the two of us. Both of us had a touching faith in its talismanic powers of protection, and it is true that for a time a symbol can outlive the plain fact that the symbol makers have turned elsewhere.

We had built our safe tower, put the trophy on the roof and dared lightning to strike. He wanted to shut out temptation. I wanted to shut it in. I wanted to be tempted by him, re-tell the story of Adam and Eve. He wanted Paradise, a sacred temenos where he would be free of his own pain. My father used to warn me, 'Never turn your back on the serpent.' He was right that the enemy of Paradise is always already inside. Jove used to laugh at my Jewishness but wasn't the serpent under the foundations of our house even then? Once or twice I caught him drinking from the buckets.

Then my husband took what was left of the stale dirty water and threw it in my face.

No escape now. I stink of it. I smell like the sluicings from the abbatoir.

He said, 'If only you would try to understand.'

I understand that pain leapfrogs over language and lands in dumb growls beyond time. A place where there is no speech and no clock, no means of separating either the moment or its misery. Nobody comes and nobody goes. It is a place unvisited by civilisation. Civilisation has not happened.

Look up at the bloody clouds made angry by the sun. Cower back from them in your nakedness and in your fear. There is no one who will help you and help is not a cry, it is still the deep ache of millennia, before humanness, before love.

The fool in his folly thinks that time before time is gone. He thinks pre-history has sunk into its swamp and we have long since drained the land and built on it. So we have, towers all, hygienic, raised up, electric lit. The horror of pre-time is a Saturday night special effects show, until I discover in my own body the swamp, the smell, the dark.

Where am I that the wind whips against the ledge battering my face and hands into the indifferent rock. No one will come to take me home. There is no home. For a little while, at least, there is sleep.

Dream. Dream myself into what I might be, out of what I have become. In the dream there is a tall mirror hinged into a case. The woman in the mirror has an unknown face. There is a sadness about her but at the side of her body, a bright light, as though the skin will burst and something alive tumble out. When I put out my hand to touch the mirror it is as warm and thin as a membrane of skin.

Do you wake up as I do, having forgotten what it is that hurts or where, until you move? There is a second of consciousness that is clean again. A second that is you, without memory or experience, the animal warm and waking into a brand new world. There is the sun dissolving the dark, and light as clear as music, filling the room where you sleep and the other rooms behind your eyes. The sun has kept his promise and risen again.

Part of you or one of you responds to this; wakes because the sun wakes, just as the earth wakes, and what can grow will. Nothing has changed this, no matter how technic, nor how remote, I go on opening my eyes to the sun.

This gives me hope. It connects me when I am most in need of connection. The grey city and its lost hearts force their way between myself and my healing. I cannot be still, wait for an answer, I can only hear the roar of the traffic and the misery under it. I am one more noise, one more pain, each locked off from the other.

Let the sun come. Break sense into nonsense. I have lain caught in the lunar crayfish night in blue waters too deep for me. I swam but there was no surface. When I fought to come up for air I came up into other waters. Where was I in the night where two dogs howled at the moon and a ruined tower reflected down at me?

In the grainy night I could not understand. Strange portents from another life opened at me. I felt delirious, absurd, these messages were unreadable or I was.

Too fast. Too soon. When a fissure opens up in the self, half-known beasts climb out of it. The sane sensible clock-driven day has been bloodied to death.

Now other laws apply and this place does not respect yours.

Nervous breakdown? Doctor, pills, rest, shh, shh. The crazy lady who frightens children. Why does she frighten children? They can still see what she sees.

'Mummy, Mummy, I saw the lady who drags the waters at her feet.'

'Don't be silly.'

I am being silly but am I any sillier than when I trusted him?

Pull yourself together.

Yes. Just pass me my leg will you? It's on top of the wardrobe where he threw it, and I think my right arm is leaning over by the wall. My head is in the gas oven but it will probably be all right, I'm told that green colour wears off. Unfortunately I threw my heart to the dogs. Never mind. No one will notice how much is missing from the inside, will they?

You look better.

Thank you. I dumped the broken bits and varnished the surface. Not bad is it? And now I can be released back into the community, encouraged to join a dating agency, and invited to speak about my experiences at a Transcendental Self-Lobotomy seminar for the prematurely smashed.

No. There is a thin line of me, wavering and not strong, that wants to learn the language of beasts and water and night. My whole self is in hiding, not daring to get too close, for the fissure smokes and belches and there are hands reaching over the edge towards me.

What is in there? The thin line is weak but curious. I have to send out my courage like a moon probe but as yet I cannot decode the incoming signal. I should have done this slowly slowly over the years. I should have learned a new language before I needed to speak it. But I never thought I needed a new language. The inner life has been just that; inner. Doesn't a healthy person look outwards? I forgot what my father said, my father in his dark coat and ringed hair, warning me to remember the serpent.

Let the sun come. I shall have to take the nights more slowly. For now it is enough to find a tiny pattern, faithfully every day, that begins to spell my name.

These matters compressed into my half-thoughts and comforted me in the second before I turned over in the half-bed. Then the gentle light of the sun was put out as my body hit a power station of pain. Is that me, voltaged out of life into one burnt smell of defeat? I read that those who are executed by electric chair retain a tiny proportion of consciousness, enough to know that they have been killed, before the final death of sense and mind.

What is the moment of death? The moment when the heart stops? The rupture of command from brain to body? The soul climbing out of its dark tower?

I come from a people to whom the invisible world is everyday present. A people for whom there is no death though death has followed them across history and continents. I come from a people who hope against hope, whose melancholy is the outer garment of their mirth. In their celebrations and in their mournings, the spirit is the same. I used to speak Yiddish and Hebrew fluently but I have not spoken either language for thirty years. What else have I lost?

The moment of death, the moment of reckoning, whatever it was, the image that stopped you, at that moment the protective accumulations of life prove useless. The inner life, the other language is what I need and the room is empty and silent.

I can't go back into the past and change it, but I have noticed that the future changes the past. What I call the past is my memory of it and my memory is conditioned by who I am now. Who I will be. The only way for me to handle what is happening is to move myself forward into someone who has handled it. As yet that person does not exist. She has not those resources. I will have to make her as Jewish legend tells how God made the first man: by moulding a piece of dirt and breathing life into it. The dirt I have in plenty. The life I will have to draw out of lungs unused to deep breathing.

What kills love? Only this: neglect.

I knew I was neglecting myself. Oh not in the ways taboo to modern religion: leaving my hair like the inside of a rabbit hutch; choosing clothes that hang as though they had started life as a horse blanket. My hands don't shake when I read the morning paper and when I take my make-up off I don't look like a red-eyed werewolf. When I put it on I don't look like a red-eyed werewolf either. I eat well, drink modestly, exercise to prevent my thighs from swimming into two seals. I read, think, work hard, and my blood pressure is average.

Was there nothing else?

There was: a woman whose face collides with mine in the mirror. I know she wants to speak to me but when she bends forward to whisper, she has no mouth.

An older woman, short and strong, dark aspect and thick hands.

When she comes close she tries to clutch me but as her hands shut around my body there is no body. I see her bent over the terrified air.

And else? A man, younger than I am. I get a feeling of him now and then when I am zipping up my jeans. He seems to want to attract attention to his balls.

When I told Jove about my occasional shadow-man, he served up Freud with the pasta and told me it was my inadequacy anxiety.

ME: I don't feel inadequate.

HE: Unconsciously you do. You need to compensate for my success.

ME: His balls are bigger than yours.

HE: Aha, but they don't exist. (He rearranged himself.)

'So when you dream of that pneumatic water-sprite, breasts a-bouncing, are you compensating for my success?'

'Hell, no, she's just a hopeless male's porno-girl. They get delivered by the breast-load.'

'And that's all?'

'That's all.'

This is the man that prises open the deepest clams of matter. Would you go fishing with him?

I did. We took a boating holiday in the Bermudas. Rocks, pale-red in the chrome water, chrome surf plating the boat.

We made a small indulgence in the dazzling austerity of the bay; its tin-tautness, the look of sheet metal, seeming to force the waves out hot-pressed not cold. The waves blistered off its smoothness, hit us with a clang and fell back again, bubbling, splitting, onto the sea tray. Perhaps we had fouled the compass and come to a magnetic pole where we were spinning, spinning in a steel sea. In the ferrousness of our situation Jove landed a fish tough as a bar.

He said, 'If we don't eat this we can use it to break into the hotel safe.'

'What's down there?'

'The fake diamonds of the fake Countess.'

'No. Down here.'

He came and lay down and stared over the edge of the boat. We could see our severed heads.

'You and me in another life.'

'Do you think we'll ever find it?'

'What's wrong with this one?' and he rolled over heating his body in the sun.

In the bow of the boat the fish panted.

I started to talk about the well and as I did so the boat becalmed itself or maybe the water tightened but we were as still and solid as a frozen boat on a frozen lake. Jove wasn't listening to me, which was as well otherwise I'm not sure I could have gone with it. It became a kind of active dreaming and the fish looked like a baton in the boat, beating time to me.

Under there, where what I am sure of is back to front, inside out, reversed, I feel in the way that I presently think, that is constantly, lucidly, testing all experience against feeling, clear and powerful as the water it suspends in.

Here, what I know by sensation, there, I know by intuition.

My empirical finger-tips numb and I can't open my eyes. What I see, what I touch is interior, either I am inside it or it is inside me. It is only vague when I subject it to the laws of the upper air. It is as though there is an entirely other way of being that makes no sense to my world, any more than my world makes sense to it. I cannot connect the two; the watery world won't move up into the dry bright light that I live in and when I take the dry bright light down there it immediately de-charges, leaving me to fumble my way in the dark.

This has been happening for years and I used to conceive of it as a poet's place or a place of inspiration; a place I imagined but where I could never actually visit. It comes closer to me than I am able to come to it. Dreams do dream us, don't they? We are not the ones in control.

Distinctly though, in the boat in the rigid sea, I had a premonition of finality. That if I did not find a way to go there soon, the seductive watery shaft would fill with rubble and I would never again approach further than its rim.

I jerked my head away and looked down the length of our little boat. Jove had fallen asleep and the fish was dead.

What is the moment of death? The hook, the line or the sinker? When I fell in love with him? When I trusted him? When he betrayed me? What kind of death is it?

I lay on the torture bed listening to its wounded springs seize as I moved. The uncoiled metal was twanging gently at the floor, a crazy lute for a crazy lover. I reached out my hand and rattled the wooden slatted blind. Lovers like music, don't they? This had been a lover's bed. I wondered if she could hear it, wherever she was, hear me, composing for her. I was no longer able to observe the steady four-four time of normal life. The rhythm didn't suit me. Perhaps it had never suited me, and I had been dancing along the way winos do, all shuffle and swank, a gin bottle Fred Astaire.

Against the rage and the self-pity and the shock was one single clear . . . thought/feeling?, that in the months before this, no, the years before this, I had heard it coming. It was like a steel ball, a ball-bearing, rolling somewhere around the apartment.

'What is that? What's come loose?' and I used to make Jove crawl round under the furniture and re-screw all the castors, and for weeks it would stop. Then, suddenly, unmistakably, across our wooden floors, the ball-bearing, rolling, rolling.

We used to joke that we had a ghost.

We did. Me.

Was it her that waits behind the mirror?

Was it her that clutches at the air and cries?

Was it him, smiling, challenging?

Was it another part of me that I had not met?

I said I had neglected myself. There's a photo of Jove and me years and years ago when we were married. He is shy, awkward, daring, defiant, the street boy pulling himself up to the avenues. I am staring out of the sensitive paper, with a look I used to have, quizzical, determined. We were new, new people in a new place and the shine was still on us.

When we killed what we were to become what we are, what did we do with the bodies? We did what most people do; buried them under the floorboards and got used to the smell.

I've lived my life like a serial killer; finish with one part, strangle it and move on to the next. Life in neat little boxes is life in neat little coffins, the dead bodies of the past laid out side by side. I am discovering, now, in the late afternoon of the day, that the dead still speak.

Past? Present? Future? The language of the dead. Totality of time.

PAGE OF SWORDS

June 8 1960. Liverpool, England. Sun in Gemini.

I was born in a tug-boat. My mother whelped me in a mess of blankets while my noctivagant father towed in the big ships.

His was the night vessel, the vessel on oily waters, his was the light shining in the darkness, come home, come home.

He worked for a shipping company and had done so since he was fifteen. He had started at the end of the war as an office boy and fourteen years later was to be made a director of the line. To celebrate he made love to my mother and I was conceived.

By day my father was a smart and increasingly smarter man. By night, or to be truthful, by three nights a week, he manned a tug-boat. There he is in a greasy donkey jacket and seaman's balaclava. Spinning the thick cable from the windlass and bringing in the banana boats, the grain boats, the boats of Turkish silver, and the boats full of Irish, shamrocks round their hearts.

When I was born the waters were still alive. My father too, was still alive, strong and burly, as wide as he was tall, with an enormous chest that looked as though it could tow the cargo boats itself.

His own family were Liverpool limeys; had always worked the docks, the boats, in the Navy or as Merchant seamen. The women had worked in the clutter of cargo offices up and down the quays. His mother, my grandmother, had been the Official Polisher of Brass Plaques and some said that when she had finished her Friday round the shine of it was so bright that it tipped the waves like a skimming stone and could still be seen in the harbour of New York.

His father, my grandfather, was killed in a war farce when an American torpedo scuppered the wrong boat. As a result, my grandmother was paid a sizeable pension and was able to have her wild strong son privately educated. She poured her money into him as though he were a treasure chest. He learned well, looked well, and if anyone questioned him about his Mersey terrace two up two down he simply knocked them out. Throughout his life my father has dealt with difficult questions by knocking them out. What is unconscious does not speak and that included the hidden part of himself.

In 1947, certificated and handsome at eighteen, he was given a lowly job-with-prospects at Trident Shipping (Progress, Tradition, Integrity). All of his family had worn clean clothes to work, that was their pride, but none had ever worn clean clothes home. For them it had been mother with a boiling hip-bath and a packet of soap flakes. My father went to work clean and he came home clean. This was an endless source of satisfaction to my grandmother who never lost her own whiff of elbow grease but delighted in the sweet smell of success.

My father loved the sea and should have been an active seaman but there were more opportunities indoors for a bright boy who had a way about him. He compensated by wheedling his way onto the tugs, and because there was still an apprenticeship mentality about the Company, his oddity was tolerated. What harm could it do and wasn't all experience useful? Besides, he did it in his own time and it made him popular with the men.

In 1957 he married my mother. She was Irish, nearly well-to-do, the daughter of a partner in the firm who was based in Cork. My father had seen her at the Annual Dinner and Dance and vowed that he would marry her. For two years they exchanged letters and gifts until romance, persistence and a promotion won the day. On their wedding night, at the Hotel Ra-Ra (décor: Merseyside-Egypt), my father took off his pyjamas so that his wife could see him man *qua* man, then told her that he would not make love to her until he had been made a director of the line. He put on his pyjamas again and after a moment or two of violent shuddering, fell asleep.

My mother lay awake pondering the matter and applied with some urgency to her father next morning. What could be done? Nothing. The young man had only recently been promoted in charge of the Atlantic crossings. He would have to prove himself there. Unfortunately he resisted all attempts by my mother to prove himself elsewhere. In despair my mother consulted my grandmother who suggested they try the Navy Position. This down-to-earth advice was not well received by my father who had already added a veneer of conventional morality to his conventional respectability.

He would not sodomise his own wife. Instead he went to New York.

There he is, built like King Kong, as ambitious as the Empire State Building, as wide-eyed as Fay Wray, and as much a dream, an invention, as the movies and America itself. He was a giant projection on the blank screen of other people and that was his success. He was not a ruthless man but he believed in himself. That marked him out from the many others who believed in nothing at all.

The dream: to pan the living clay that you are and find gold in it. Perhaps my father was a treasure chest because he seemed to be able to lay up for himself inexhaustible riches. Whatever he tried succeeded. He should have been a Venetian merchant pacing the Rialto. He should have been Marco Polo winning furs out of Muscovy. Is that him, on the log rafts in Quebec? Is that him riding rapids with the snow mantling his shoulders? He was a man who belonged with an elk, with a moose. A whale man, a bear man. Instead he wore a loose suit and a trilby and learned how to net a profit. His hauls were the biggest in the Company and he turned them in like a little boy. In those days his true self was still fighting with his assumed self, and winning. Person and persona, the man and his mask had separate identities then, he knew which was which. Later, the man my mother married died before his death and the man who had come to be his counterfeit wore his clothes.

But that was in the future, and in 1959 my father was in the fullness of his present, he could do no wrong.

It was a shining morning, he was leaning on the harbourside rail, watching the cranes load the ships. The world poured through his fingers; spices, wine, tea, green bananas, coconuts, American golf clubs, blankets made of wool with satin hemmed round the edges.

Today they were loading nylon stockings, Monroe look-alikes stamped all over the cardboard boxes.

The wind was warm, trade wind with generosity and travel in it, a wind to scatter the ships to the four corners of the earth and although my father was too young for ships with sails, like other water-men, the wind still excited him. A fair wind. A new world. The recklessness of the sailor that my father loved.

These were his happiest times, the times when his paperwork was done, when he could hear his secretary rattling at the upright Remington as though it were a church piano. He worked evenings and early mornings so that he could make a gap to slip through, a private space after coffee and before lunch, when the piers were busy with every kind of activity, legitimate and not.

He knew the gangmen and the loaders and the truck drivers and the harbour pilots, and as he leaned on his rail, watching, sometimes waving, other men joined him, lit a cigarette, told him the news and with a slap on the back, moved on. The easy fraternity of working men was comfortable to him. No one here asked him what school he had attended.

As he gossiped and lounged the noise of the Remington stopped. His secretary came out from the low line of offices that huddled to the waterfront. There was an urgent call for him. Would he step inside at once?

Sighing, he threw down his cigarette and went inside, straightening his tie. He listened briefly. 'Yes. Yes.' Then he threw down the receiver and threw his secretary up into the air.

He had been made a Director of the Line.

He left his desk with its four black telephones and filing tray, and without stopping to collect any luggage, bought an aeroplane ticket for the evening flight. In 1959 flying was odd, glamorous, expensive and blissful. There was a fifteen-minute check-in time and my father walked across the tarmac and boarded the twin-propeller plane with only his toothbrush to declare.

He had risen in the world and now he was going to prove it.

When he arrived home my mother was not expecting him. His secretary had not made the instructed call. Mother was in the bath, with bubbles up to her neck, and my grandmother, on the bath-stool, was reading out loud from the Bible. This was their regular Sunday visiting hour, and having little in common and less to say, they had hit on the happy idea of spiritual elevation. My mother never listened to what my grandmother read, but she felt she was doing her duty by her family and by God, and it saved her the trouble of going to church. My grandmother, who was firmly convinced by the Word of the Lord, took more pleasure in that hour than in any other of the week, including 2 p.m. Thursday when she drew her pension.

They had begun with Genesis and were now at the Book of Job, with whose trials my grandmother sympathised, especially since she had recently developed a boil.

As she read 'Who will avail me in my tribulation?' the door flew open and my father reached down into the bath and scooped out my mother whole and carried her off into the bedroom.

My grandmother, who was not a nervous type, said to herself, 'David must have got his promotion.' Nodding, she finished the chapter, let out the bath water and trudged home.

Meanwhile, in a maze of soggy sheets and copies of *Woman's Weekly*, my father speared my mother on his manhood.

'I should have tidied up first,' she said.

'Harpoon Ahoy!' said my father.

And somewhere in all this I was.

On the night of my birth my father got the madness on him and told my mother he had to go tugging.

'I'll come with you,' she said. 'I feel well.'

Accordingly, my father put on his Jolly Jack Tars and my mother wrapped herself up in her mink coat. In those days their car was a three-litre Rover, really, a leather three-piece suite and cocktail cabinet on wheels. My father purred down to the docks looking like a criminal, while my mother fixed herself a strictly forbidden gin and tonic in the back.

When they reached the docks my father backed into a loading bay and my grandmother stepped out of the shadows.

'David,' she said.

She was wearing a black oilskin that had been her husband's. It hung on her from head to foot, so much so that she seemed less to be wearing a rainproof than to be in the grip of a monster from the Deep.

'Is something wrong?' said my father.

'Tha wife's to give birth.'

'Oh not yet,' said my mother.

'Yet,' said the Oilskin.

And so the three of them climbed aboard the *Godspeed* and chugged into the dark.

On board my grandmother unpacked her carpet bag. She set out a pile of clean rags, the ones she used for polishing the brass plaques, a bottle of cooking brandy, a bottle of iodine, a primus stove, a cylinder of water, a kitchen knife, a packet of sandwiches, a little blanket from the dog's box, her spectacles and the Bible, now open towards the end of the Psalms. This done, she took off her oilskin and pegged it over the hatch.

'David shan't like it,' she said.

'I'm quite sure that it will be at least a week before the birth,' said my mother who immediately went into labour.

My mother. Miss 1950s. The perfect post-war wife. She was pretty, she was charming, she was clever enough but not too, she smiled at the men and gave the women that quizzical bewildered look, as if to say, 'What, am I not the only one then?'

Her stocking seams were straight, her hair was curled, her back was upright, her waist was curved, her legs were long, her breasts round, her stomach was flat, her bottom was not. Black hair, blue eyes, red mouth, pale skin, and all this packed as neatly as picnic Tupperware. There was nothing of the whore about her and this my father liked.

She had been well educated and taught to conceal it. She never gave up singing and playing the piano and she never gave up her watercolours. The rest of the mind she disposed of at marriage and did not think to ask my father what he had done with it.

She was not resourceful; her class did not allow it, and I know it worried my grandmother that her son had found a wife who did not know how to make a soup out of herrings' heads.

My father no longer wanted herring heads. He wanted mink and pearls and he got them. Like most men he was a transvestite at one remove; if his wife was part of him so were her clothes. She was his rib and as such he too wore a silk shift. He loved her clothes, loved to see her dressed up, it satisfied a part of him that was deeper than vanity. It was a part of himself. She completed him. She manifested him at another level. He absorbed her while she failed to absorb him. This was so normal that nobody noticed it. At least not until later, much later, when things began to change.

Husband and wife. Man and rib. What could be more normal than that? And now they were having a baby. That is, my mother was bearing my father's child. It was different when my sisters were born but I was Athene.

Athene born fully formed from the head of Zeus.

The legend says that Zeus lusted after a Titan called Metis and eventually got her with child. An oracle told Zeus that the baby would be a girl but that if Metis ever conceived again, she would bear a boy who would overthrow Zeus, just as Zeus had deposed his own father, Kronos. In fear, Zeus stroked and flattered Metis until she came close enough to kiss him of her own free will. He swallowed her.

Months later, proud complacent Zeus had a headache and yowled his way over the earth, threatening to split the firmament with pain. It was Hermes who told him the source of his trouble, and Hephaestus, the lame god of the smithy who took a hammer and wedge and split open Lord Zeus's skull. Out came Athene tall strong beautiful and her father's own.

No one will doubt that my father had wanted a boy. He had assumed he would have a boy. Right up to a week after my birth he continued to say, 'How is he?' My grandmother told me that he had turned me upside down in his huge hands and held me V-legged to the light, just to be sure that my genitals weren't caught inside. He didn't trust doctors. The white coat and stethoscope seemed to him to be a hide-out from the world. He resented the superiority, the authority, but of course he had never been ill.

When he stopped holding me up to the light he began to hold me up to the mirror.

He wanted to compare us, side by side, did I look like him?

He had been taught to hold my head and to support my unfixed spine, and I seem to remember sitting solemnly on his level palm, trying to steady the out of focus vision of him, anxious, intent, gazing at me as if I could reveal to him what he was.

He slept in his dressing room for the first couple of months. After my mother had fed me, sometime around 5 a.m., she would fall into a deep sleep and my father used to creep in and pick me up in his huge hands and take me to his room where the fire glowed. Perhaps it was there, held by him, in front of the mirror, the strange room in reflection behind, that I came to imagine other places, glowing steadily, just out of reach.

'I christen this child . . .'

Poor baby, passed from hand to hand like a pouch of tobacco, a fresh-faced narcotic promising hope, change, at least for now. My family are addicted to sentimentality. If that sounds cruel it is only the cruelty of too close observation for too long. Unable to express their feelings in the normal course of days and hours they need every legitimate excuse to do so. They cannot say 'I love you' so they say 'Isn't she lovely?' 'Well done.' They can seem like bon viveurs, always a party in the offing, my mother planning a new recipe for canapés even in the act of stuffing my relatives with the ones she has just made.

It should have been fun but neither of them was happy. When I was five my father was on pills and my mother was on gin. I think I was happy, in the maddening determined way that children have of being happy, and it was that happiness that worked as a magnet on both of my parents. They were pulled by it, they wanted it, and instead of taking it for granted, they started to take it to bits.

'Are you happy, Alice?'

'Yes, Daddy.'

'Why?' And he would stare at me in that way of his, trying to see happiness the way he could see a business opportunity.

On my sixth birthday the parties started. I had a cake, presents, a new frock. The adults had what my father called a '*foie gras*'. How much can you eat and drink without vomiting over the coffee table?

Neither my mother nor my father were able to cope with the 1960s. Skirts were too short, hair was too long, and the favoured colour combination of purple and orange made my mother look like a vampire and my father a Matisse. They were peculiarly ill-placed for the general assault on the past that the Sixties represented because they lived in Liverpool. Liverpool, that should have slumbered its way through the Sixties as it had every other decade, produced the Beatles. My parents were victims of the Merseybeat.

One day when my mother was taking me to school, the streets seemed very quiet. We parked, although we were the only car on the stretch of road, and we got out to walk slowly, hand in hand, through some flimsy barriers of paper and string. Far away we saw some policemen waving at us and we waved back. We heard a lorry coming up behind and my mother told me it had a television crew on board which excited me who had never seen a television. Anything that had been on the market for as little as ten years was unlikely to impress my father.

As the lorry came close to us, four young men dressed entirely in black ran past. Three of them carried guitars, one had a set of drumsticks. I had seen people dressed in black before.

'Is it a funeral?' I asked my mother.

She didn't answer. She was looking back down the road. Suddenly she picked me up and shot at full pelt back to our car. I didn't know my mother could run. I had never seen her run. She threw me in the back seat and flung herself in after me in a whirl of Dior and hairpins.

At that second the car was rocked on every side by thousands of screaming girls. I saw their faces streaked with tears pressed in agony against the windows and windscreen of the car. It can hardly have lasted a moment; they realised their prey was elsewhere and vanished as devilishly as they had appeared. When my mother got out to talk to the policeman, the only trace of what had happened was a broken banner painted HELP!

'Mob rule,' said my father who was thinking of moving to Southampton.

I was strictly forbidden to listen to the Beatles and Beatles music was strictly forbidden at the now monthly parties my parents held for anyone who would come. I began to dread the parties; the unknown women who would come upstairs to cry in a spare bedroom. The drunk and drunker men who used to talk about the war and hold each other's knees. I persuaded my parents to let me go and stay with my grandmother on party nights. My mother was reluctant because she thought that my grandmother was unhygienic. There was no foundation to this, only my grandmother's absolute refusal to fit an inside toilet or to attend any of my mother's Tupperware evenings.

As I was ready to go with my nightcase packed, my mother gave me a bottle of disinfectant. 'For the out-house,' she said. 'Don't tell Grandmother.' Don't tell Grandmother. My grandmother had been an honorary member of the secret police since she was born. It was impossible to hide anything from her. As I came through the back door into her kitchen she frisked me from head to foot, removed the disinfectant and gave me a pair of overalls to wear. 'Help me clean out the toilet,' she said.

For the first time in months I felt my body slacken. I had been carrying myself like a gun, cocked, alert, ready for trouble, fearing it. My parents were rowing and when they weren't rowing they were snapping and when they weren't snapping they were planning a party, holding a party, clearing up after a party. Here, shovelling human compost out of my grandmother's cloaca, I was happy again. We stacked the rich mould around her roses and she sang me ballads from the docks, easing her voice with regular swigs from an unmarked tin-billy. 'Grog-blossom,' she said tapping her nose the colour of the roses.

Her kitchen had strings of onions and fat hams hanging in glorious torture from twisted hooks in the ceiling. She smoked her own kippers up the chimney, skewering them in pairs with discarded knitting needles. For this she kept a wood fire. The other fireplaces were fed on coal. She had a glass-fronted cabinet lined with jars of homemade preserve; pickles, tomatoes, pears, cabbage, and in the middle, a baby rabbit. This was not for eating. It was an ornament. When the wind blew and the cupboard rattled the rabbit bobbed up and down in his transparent prison, his ears buckling slightly as they hit the lid seal.

The furniture was plain: a scrubbed sycamore table, a deep

enamel sink, a few unmatched chairs and an evil-smelling coal Rayburn that left soot on my grandmother's scones.

'Won't hurt,' said Grandmother. 'Look at me.'

Yes, look at her, bunioned, bulbous, hair in bulrush rolls, butt-headed, butter-hearted and tenacious as a buckaroo.

When she ate her scones she left a snail-trail of soot along her upper lip. Her neighbour called her 'Blackmouth'. My grandmother called her neighbour 'Stinkpad' but otherwise they were friendly, exchanging handkerchiefs and soap at Christmas.

My grandmother got down a pair of kippers and broiled them for us in butter and water. She asked me about my father, watching my body not listening to what I said, what could I say? I loved him and he frightened me. 'My mistake,' she said talking to herself. 'My mistake.'

And if she was thinking of the school, or his first job in a collar and tie while his mates were at the boats, or the ordinary girl who had loved him, or her own pride, she never told me, then or at any time. Like my father she could not speak what she felt. Unlike him she knew this and sat many hours with her head in her hands, I thought then, to make the words fall out. But the words did not fall out and her feelings hung inside her, preserved.

When we had finished scooping out the dunny, and put fresh sawdust in the bottom to activate the new midden, my grandmother said she had a surprise for me. She made me stand in the corner of the kitchen behind the memorial oilskin, while she wheezed and whirred something out of the coal-hole. I could hear a crackling and a scratching and what sounded like fluff on the end of a record-player needle.

'Come out,' said Grandmother.

On the kitchen table was a brand-new bright blue Dansette

turntable. On the turntable was a 45r.p.m. of the Beatles singing 'Help!'

Whilst I was adjusting to this unlikely apparition, my grand-mother was doing the Twist or perhaps it would be better to say the Wiggle, since the two mobile parts were her bottom and her head. Her arms, bent at the elbow, were rigid in front of her, her feet were planted apart.

'I'll teach you,' she said.

She did teach me and we did not tell my mother or my father about the privy or the scones or the dancing lessons or the unnamed grog or the teenage turntable in its vinyl zip case or the happiness that was unhygienic or the sense of peace that had the smell of buttered kippers.

'You must be bored there,' said my mother.

My parents' house was so clean it made me ill. Much has been aired about the benefits of sanitation but less is told about the eczema of washing powder, the asthma of fitted carpets, allergic reactions to cream cleaner, itchy fingers round the bleach bottle, drug-out on the fumes of metal polish. Worse, my mother had dis-covered nylon, so easy to wash, and ignored my athlete's foot and the red weals between my legs where the nylon lace of the nylon knickers warred against my non-nylon skin.

It would have been better if I had been made of nylon; easier then to soak out the miseries that were soaking in.

I grew. At nine, tall and silent, I was unhappy. My father, who had given up his religion but not the superstition that accompanied it, interpreted my misery as proof positive of Original Sin. Since there could be no reason for me to be unhappy, unhappiness must be the human condition. How could he hope to escape what an innocent child could not escape? Like my grandmother, he had a Gothic disposition, but she had kept her God and therefore her mercy. My father could find no mercy for himself and offered none.

As his world darkened, the shadows in our house increased. We lived in a big light spacious well-windowed generous house, designed by Lutyens. My father had bought it for my mother in a grand gesture of love and pride. Not for her a poky terrace with a dog kennel and an outside toilet. The garden shrubbed and green had a noose of trees all round it and in the centre of the rolled lawn was a Victorian sun-dial of granite and slate. At the bottom of the dial was the hooded figure of Time scything the hours, but at the top, over the position of the twelve was an angel with a trumpet bearing the inscription '*Aliquem alium internum*'. I did not know what this meant and when I was able to translate it I did not understand it. Later it came to mean a great deal to me but that is not yet.

When the hours were golden and green it seemed as if the whole house levitated. My father pleased with his work, my mother pleased with her home and her children. I don't remember the exact moment of the eclipse, only a gradual chilliness and the golden light paling yellow-pale-yellow-yellow to fade. I do remember that my father felt cheated. His salary was insufficient, his bonus was insufficient, his challenges were puny, his achievements were not fully recognised. He said those things to my mother, I heard him, but to me he said, by the sun-dial, 'I'm forty-one and the sea is dying.' He ran his finger back and forth over the hooded Time.

In my nightmares Time scooped up the sea in his hood and carried it away. He stood at the end of the world and poured the sea into space.

The glittering fish were stars.

It was inevitable that the air should fight its war with the sea. Cargo and passengers alike preferred to fly and as shipping costs increased air prices dropped. My father's company, man and boy, was suffering unsustainable losses. Trident Shipping, founded 1809, was slowly going bankrupt and taking my father with it.

He had enough money. It was his life they were draining away. His friends interpreted his resentment as a normal response to a difficult situation. My mother took the simple view that a man must have his work. My father though, was not simple and he was still aware enough to turn the mask over and over in his hands and ask what it was. Uncharacteristically, he went to visit my grandmother.

'What have I made of my life?'

'David you've got everything you wanted.'

'What did I want?'

'Didn't you want to be somebody?'

'Didn't you?'

Yes. No. The clock ticking and the smell of buttered kippers. The young man out of his mother's body and wearing his father's clothes. Be someone. Be someone. Redeem history. Make our lives not an endless sacrifice but a gathering of energy, the strength to jump, but we fall, the strength to jump, but we fall, until you who leap and do not fall. Then we see what we were for, the single stuttered words gain the momentum of narrative. This is the story of a humble family who became a name. My son David whose father grandfather and great-grandfather unto the sixth generation worked the docks. My son David, rich, respected, powerful, a man. My son David whose eyes have the shine in them. My son David pulling history home.

'Mother?'

'David.'

They did not speak of it again. My father took his hat and scarf and walked down to the docks. There were men there he knew, idle like him, and they envied him his money and although he was not stupid enough to envy them their poverty, there was part of him that regretted all he had done. They drank together. He drank alone. He wanted to go with them to the filthy Admiral Arms but what right had he to sit in his cups when they would be going home to cheap rations and unpaid bills? He desperately wanted to say, 'I am unhappy.' How could he say that to them?

He didn't come home that night, nor the night after. The telephone rang each evening at six o'clock until a week had passed. My mother looked vaguer than usual and kept her light on all night. We were supposed not to notice. Now that it was winter the house was dark almost all day and the frost whitened the lawn. My sisters and I played quietly in the petrified air, our breath briefly warming the frozen spaces around us. We were waiting, waiting, watching the clock.

On the sixth day of his absence my mother appeared in the dining room, in her mink coat, carrying a small suitcase. The three of us were doing a jigsaw while the inadequate fire tried to melt the icicles that were hanging in long spears around the room.

'I have to go to your father,' she said and kissed us with her cold red mouth. 'Grandmother will be here.'

Grandmother was here, wrapped from head to foot in woollens, her face entirely obscured by a seaman's balaclava. She made us a cup of cocoa and my mother swept off in a taxi.

'Where has she gone?'

'London,' said my grandmother, pronouncing it Hell.

'There's no sea there is there?'

I felt that my father had gone to his death.

I helped Grandmother unpack her things; a week's supply of kippers and her Bible. I opened it at the marker and found that we were back at the Book of Job. This meant my grandmother was in tribulation, though on this occasion her tribulation had a kind of glittering intensity about it that heated the indifferent house and made us excited again. Very often she said, 'The horse that crieth among the trumpets Aha!' and I wondered what kind of a horse it was that would do that. Undeterred, we imitated him and soon the zero house was filled with smells and smoke and voices crying Aha!

I said, 'If we were good always would we be happy always?'

'No,' said Grandmother.

'Then I shall be bad.'

'Where's the difficulty in that?'

The difficulty. Something in her, something in him, something that I inherited that my sisters did not. The horse that crieth among the trumpets Aha! Why wrestle all night with an angel when the fight can only leave you lame? Why not walk away? Why not sleep?

My grandmother loved me because she recognised the same stubbornness that she had gened in her son. The difficulty and the dream were not separate. To pan the living clay that you are is to stand in the freezing waters and break yourself on a riddle of your own making. No one can force you to it. No one can force you away. Rhinegold, pure gold and somewhere in the Rhinegold, the ring.

Later, much later when I heard Wagner's *Ring* cycle I thought of the times when I had been a very little child and my father had taken me to watch the sunset on the estuary. He loved the gold light dabbling the water. His mind played in it. He and his images were still free but then the moving gold hardened around him and he began to count it. The stories agree that in the difficulty and the dream the hero should never count the cost.

There was a terrific rattling and thundering at the door and my mother and father burst into the hall; she in a silver fox, he in a new overcoat and trilby. Behind them, a taxi-driver struggled up the steps with a pile of boxes.

My father swung us up in his arms and laughed and said we were going on an adventure.

'We're going to live in London,' he said.

'Why Daddy?'

'Because Daddy has a new job.'

My father had heard that Cunard, the most illustrious and prestigious shipping line in the United Kingdom, was to be bought up by Trafalgar House Investments. Cunard had recently taken delivery of their new flagship, the *QE2*, and were making money on her. My father had been to the launch party in Southampton and met a few men he liked and who had liked him. Two of them had been to one of his *foie gras* parties. One of them had suggested he might consider a key role in the reorganisation of the Cunard enterprise, with particular responsibility for the *QE2*'s Atlantic crossings. For my father it seemed like the dream again, youth again, just married again, a place where the sea was still alive and where he too would be alive. Cunard's headquarters were in London and in a matter of weeks so were we.

★

Before we left we went to see my headmaster. I had just started secondary school and was restless and inattentive. The headmaster, noting that I had every advantage life could offer, assumed that I was either a bad child or a dull one. He was too afraid of my rugger-square father to use either of those words, at least I know that now, but at the time I believed he meant what he said. For the next eight years I lived shut away in the misery of his drawer.

There were compensations. Now that I was officially not clever my father began to take me with him on his business trips. He reckoned that if I could not benefit from an expensive education I could perhaps benefit from experience. My sisters were sent to board at Benenden, I went to the local Catholic school, from whose piety and Home Economics lessons I was frequently removed to accompany my father. In 1973, when I was thirteen, we flew to New York to join the *QE2* on a Comet Watch. It was this that constellated my future.

The idea, his idea, was a three-day cruise to chase the comet Kohoutek, named after the Czech astronomer who had discovered it. It was expected to be one of the brightest comets of the twentieth century, and in some ways the cruise was the beginning of millennium fever. Religion may lose its appeal but portents are popular. The sell-out cruise, itself something of a *foie gras*, was packed with atheists looking for mystery. Unfortunately the weather was so bad that most of the adults found their best visions in a champagne bottle. My father was very busy and I was left alone.

It was night, about a quarter to twelve, the sky divided in halves, one cloudy, the other fair. The stars were deep recessed, not lying on the surface of the night but hammered into it. The water, where the ship cutted it, was broken and white, but once the ship had passed the water healed the intrusion and I could not see where the black of the sky and the black of the water changed into each other. I thought of my often-dream where Time poured the fishes into the sky and the sky was full of star fish; stella maris of the upper air. There are many legends among seafaring people of a bright fish so hot that it shines in the deepest water, a star dropped and finned from God, an alchemical mystery, the union of fire and water, *coniuntis oppositorum* that transforms itself and others. Some writers mix the stella maris with the remora, a tiny fish that sticks to the rudder of a vessel and brings it to a halt. Whatever it is, the fateful decisive thing that utterly alters a confident course.

My father had told me about the remoras and how the Greek fishermen in the little boats still fear him. My father feared no remoras.

Dog. Dog-fish. Dog star.

Horse. Sea-horse. Pegasus.

Monk. Monk fish. Angel.

Spider. Spider-crab. Cancer.

Worm. Eel. The Old Serpent.

I was at the age of making lists but the lists I made were correspondences, half true and altogether fanciful, of the earth the sea and the sky. Perhaps I was trying to hold together my own world that was in so much danger of falling away. Perhaps I wanted order where there was none. As the *QE2* floated so confidently on the waters I thought of the *Titanic*, ghostly and abandoned beneath, and somewhere above, in the secretive blackness, the Ship of Fools navigating the stars. Was it the comet?

Legend has it that the Ship, while seeking the Holy Grail, sailed off the end of the world and continued forever. At particular conjunctions of time and timelessness, it appears again as a bright light, shooting its course through the unfathomable universe, chasing that which has neither beginning nor end.

What can a little girl see that astronomers and telescopes cannot? There was no comet sighted on the official log of the journey. What was it then that hooped together ordinary night with infinity? I saw the silver prow pass over me and the sails in tattered cloth. Men and women crowded at the deck. There was a shuddering, as though the world-clock had stopped, though in fact it was our own ship that had thrown its engines into reverse. In the morning my father told me that we had identified an unknown signal, thought to be a vessel just ahead of us, though nothing at all was found.

For myself, in the dark, watching the thin silver line speed away, I had joined that band of pilgrims uncenturied, unquantified, who, call it art, call it alchemy, call it science, call it god, are driven by a light that will not stay.

The *Godspeed*. My father at the wheel. My mother on a hard couch giving birth to me.

My mother lay with her skirts up over her face, her perfect stockings round her ankles, her pain groaning against the heavy noise of the engine.

My head was engaged and I was pushing out of my mother's chthonic underworld into my father's world of difficulty and dream. I never expected to go back down again.

My grandmother was singing a hymn, essentially praising God but effectively preventing my father from hearing what was happening. It was a quick birth and when I was laid on my mother's breast, my grandmother ate a sandwich and went to tell my father that he had the pleasure of a daughter.

He lit every one of his distress flares and burnt up the river in a blaze of phosphorous red. Every tug and patrol boat on the stretch surrounded us, but far from sinking we were celebrating. My grandmother called it the Miracle of the Sardines and the Gin. She had only fetched enough for herself but there seemed to be plenty for everyone and so I was born, in dirt, in delight, in water and in spirits, with fish above and below and under an exacting star.

THE STAR

November 10 1947. City of New York. Sun in Scorpio.

Papa was a bookseller in Vienna. Mama designed posters for the Austrian railway. There was nothing extraordinary about my parents before World War Two, only that Mama was German and Papa was Jewish.

'*Der Paß wird ungültig am 24 März 1939 wenn er nicht verlängert wird.*'

'If not extended, this passport will expire by March 24 1939.' On the first page of the Reisepass, inside the blood-brown cover, was a blood-bright 'J'.

Papa had friends in New York, and it was his friends who arranged his papers so that he could travel before his passport expired and while he still had funds. The authorities were ready crouched to confiscate his goods, his business, his house, his wife.

As a German, Mama would have been granted an immediate divorce.

This is the odd thing: my parents were not happily married. Mama was out of love with Papa. Papa was sunk in his books. When he left for the steamer to New York, Mama need never have seen him again.

What did she do?

She applied for a separate passport which was granted. She filed for divorce, which won her the approval of the authorities, and of her Catholic priest, Father Rohr. While he instructed her in the Church's view of the Jewish Question, she flirted with a high-ranking Nazi officer, and let him indulge her in selling off as much of Papa's property as she could. She smelted the price into gold belts.

When she had done as much as she dared to do, she excused herself from her lover and her job on the pretext of a short holiday to visit her father in Bavaria. In fact, she took a train to Switzerland, crossed into France and met the boat to New York. She walked slowly, weighed down as she was with a belt of gold ingots strapped under her dress.

Had she been discovered she would have been shot.

She had her own job, she was German, she could have married again and married well. She had never thought of herself as political. Why did she risk her life for a man from whom she had longed to be free?

It was an extravagant gesture and one of unpredicted alchemical success. The trodden clay of their marriage was transformed into a noble bolus. Out of time, for a time, they flourished.

Papa opened a bookshop on Amsterdam Avenue by 75th St. He

sold anything second hand, and it was there that I began to read literature and poetry and the texts of the Kabbalah, often taking books back home, slowly crossing the Park, to read them on the fire escape of our apartment building, while the courting couples sang to one another in Yiddish.

'The child squints,' said Mama when I was born.

'She will be a poet,' said Papa, who was a student of physiognomy.

> A Knife and Fork
> A Bottle and a Cork
> That's the way to spell
> New York.

That was the first poem that I learned by heart from a child whose father sold bagels. Mama despaired and bought me an illuminated copy of Faust. Papa said, 'Look up.'

Not at the skyscrapers being built overnight from nothing out of Manhattan bedrock. Not at the fierce cranes preying over the sky. He said, 'Every blade of grass that grows here on earth has its corresponding influence in the stars. This is the Mazalot.'

He said, 'Intensity is the Desire to Receive. Open yourself to light and you will become light.'

I did not understand my mystical Papa, who each morning bound on tefillin, the small black boxes containing portions of the Torah which would contain and direct his energy.

'Is it magic?' I asked Mama, who shrugged and seemed to find no spells in the stacks of aluminium pots and pans burnt with food she didn't like to cook.

My Teutonic Mama, Brünnhilde in her belly, her own spell the ring of fire that surrounded her. No man could approach. She was the woman on the burning rock, waiting, waiting, for the hero who would be worthy of her. It was not my Papa. Hadn't she been the one to rescue him? And so the dream burned.

New York was pulling itself up by its own pigtail. In those days, after the war, cement mixers used to trawl around the city, ready to jack their load at a whistle from a gang-man. Higher up, on the steel frames of the giant buildings, men with monkey courage tossed red-hot rivets into steel buckets. We were bolting together the future. Rich and poor alike, the rivets of a new world.

I read William Wordsworth: 'Bliss was it in that dawn to be alive,/ But to be young was very heaven.'

I read William Blake: 'How do you know but every bird that cuts the airy way/Is an immense world of delight, closed by your senses five?'

I read Whitman: 'I moisten the roots of all that has grown.'

The streets. The cross-streets. The Hudson river where the cattle came up on freight trains. The smell of the abbatoir. The smell of cement. Hot metal. Hot bagels. Cold water on the new-cast buildings. The courtyard of our apartment block. The dark young men, deep eyed, nesting on the shelves of our bookstore. Mama in her dress of red polka dots outside the Woolworth Building. The long coats of the old Russian Jews. Fresh grated horseradish. Schapiro's 'Wines you can almost cut with a knife'. Papa's yellowing copies of the *Jewish Daily Forward*. Our upright piano. The chauffeurs dressed in double-breasted jackets and leather leggings in Central Park. Papa, walking, walking, the twelve and a half miles along, two and a half miles wide of this Aladdin island where anyone might be lucky enough to turn up a magic lamp.

Papa's friends were in the Lower East Side, piled-up streets of Jewish busyness, where thin men with dybbuks in their eyes gave me challah bread to eat while they sold water-stained books to Papa, who carried them to the store in a huge carpet bag.

Mama's friends on the Upper East Side, all Germans, with unfinishable supplies of pea and ham broth and whopper sausage. Mama in her neat feather hat and buttoned suit. Mama and her secret promise that one day we would go back to Vienna or maybe Berlin.

The years fold up neatly into single images, single words, and what went between was like a glue or a resin that held the important things in place, until, now, later, when they stand alone, the rest decayed, leaving certain moments as time's souvenirs.

Should it daunt me that the things I thought would be important, my list of singularities and tide marks, is as useless as the inventory of a demolished house? I no longer recognise the urgency of my old diaries with their careful recording of what mattered. What I wrote down is in another person's handwriting. What has held me are the things I did not say, the things I put away. What returns, softly, or in floods, disturbs me by its newness. Its vividness. What returns are not the well-worn memories I have carefully recorded, but spots of time that badge me out as the dull red J did Papa. I am marked by those stubborn parts of me.

Perhaps I did know it would be so. I remember walking with Papa on one of his dogged night leads, after some book or other, and coming up into Times Square just as the lights were switched off. Papa, guided by the Light Within, strode on unperturbed.

I, in the second's translation from brilliantness to nothingness, felt the world disappear. And if it could disappear so easily, what was it?

'Shadows, signs, wonders,' said Papa.

I read Whitman: 'The sense of what is real, the thought if after all it should prove unreal.'

Against Papa's Kabbalah, his worship at the Temple Emanu-el on Fifth Avenue, his strange friendships and the visits of the cantors, Mama set her Germanness. She was not a mystic, though her real quarrel with Papa's more arcane experiments was that he undertook them in her saucepans. She did not want to fry her latkes over the remains of a potion to restrain klippot (demons, shells, evil husks, whatever separates man from G-d).

Her father had been a butcher, a lapsed Catholic turned cleaver atheist, 'When I chop this up where is the soul?' She had disliked his Bavarian brutality and moved to Vienna to study painting and drawing, supporting herself by selling lightning sketches in cafés. She had been timidly intellectual and attracted to Papa because he made vast systems out of nothing. Her religion was faint, his was hidden. He seemed to be fleeing his Jewishness, and only a few years after they were married did he begin to study Kabbalah, late night, burnt-eyed. As he turned inwards she turned outwards, but while he wore his intensity like a garment, she slept in hers. Both denied what was real to the other. To her he was mad. To him she was cold.

For a little while, in New York, they remembered each other for each other. They were happy. Then both began to warm themselves at different fires.

Into this unlikely blaze came their child. Squint-eyed. Poetical. The one defect of vision has corrected itself. And the other?

Defect of vision. Do I mean affect of vision? At the beginning of the twentieth century when Picasso, Matisse, and Cézanne were turning their faces towards a new manner of light, there was a theory spawned by science and tadpoled by certain art critics that frog-marched the picture towards the view that this new art was an optical confusion. Nothing but a defect of vision. The painters were astigmatic; an abnormality of the retina that unfocuses rays of light. That was why they could not paint realistically. They could not see that a cat is a cat is a cat.

Recently I heard the same argument advanced against El Greco. His elongations and foreshortenings had nothing to do with genius, they were an eye problem.

Perhaps art is an eye problem; world apparent, world perceived. Signs, shadows, wonders.

What you see is not what you think you see.

Papa in the dark room above the bookstore, waiting for the fifteenth of the month when the moon would be full. Papa with his stones of topaz. What was the light that shone in the darkness? What was the stone-glow, the living asterisk that made the bare room into a battery, Papa's holy voltaic cell. Climb the stairs and listen outside the door to his half-singing, half-chanting, a thin wire of sound connecting him to the encircling light, the Or Makif, that must be drawn in.

Climb the stairs. Mama in the shop below making order out of the piles of books dumped by Papa, exhausted, excited, after another night's walking to mekubalim behind hidden doors.

Mama on her little wooden ladder, seams straight, Count Basie

on the radio, the slight swing of her bottom, and the lamp showing her underslip beneath her blouse.

Papa, his parchments, his gems, his dark lit-up face.

Mama, blonde and blue, gold-fingered and almost still.

I was afraid. I ran outside.

Mama said, 'Watch where you go.'

Papa said, 'What you see is not what you think you see.'

Defect of vision. Do I mean affect of vision?

'Science cannot solve the ultimate mystery of nature because
we ourselves are part of nature and therefore part of the mystery we are trying to solve.'   (Max Planck)

'It appears unavoidable that physical reality must be described
in terms of continuous functions in space. The material point
can hardly be conceived anymore.'   (Albert Einstein)

'If we ask whether the position of the electron remains the
same we must say no. If we ask whether the electron's position
changes with time, we must say no. If we ask whether the electron is at rest we must say no. If we ask whether it is in motion
we must say no.'   (Robert Oppenheimer)

Is truth what we do not know?

What we know does not satisfy us. What we know constantly
reveals itself as partial. What we know, generation by generation, is
discarded into new knowings which in their turn slowly cease to
interest us.

In the Torah, the Hebrew 'to know', often used in a sexual

context, is not about facts but about connections. Knowledge, not as accumulation but as charge and discharge. A release of energy from one site to another. Instead of a hoard of certainties, bug-collected, to make me feel secure, I can give up taxonomy and invite myself to the dance: the patterns, rhythms, multiplicities, paradoxes, shifts, currents, cross-currents, irregularities, irrationali-ties, geniuses, joints, pivots, worked over time, and through time, to find the lines of thought that still transmit.

The facts cut me off. The clean boxes of history, geography, science, art. What is the separateness of things when the current that flows each to each is live? It is the livingness I want. Not mummification. Livingness. I suppose that is why I fell in love with Jove. Or to be accurate, why I knew I would fall in love with Jove, when I first saw him, on the day that I was born.

Energy precedes matter.

The day I was born.

It was a cold snowy winter New York. Cold was master. Heat was servant. Cold landlorded it in every tenement block, pushing the heat into smaller and smaller corners, throwing the heat out onto the streets where it disappeared in freezes of steam. No one could get warm. Furnaces and boilers committed suicide under the strain and were dragged lifeless from the zero basements by frozen men in frozen overalls. The traffic cops, trying to keep order in the chaos-cold, felt their semaphoring arm stiffen away from their bodies. It was a common sight, at shift change, to see them lifted like statues off their podiums, and laid horizontal in a wheezing truck.

The cars and wagons and trolley buses moved slower and

slower, valves faltering, carburettors icing, until with a protesting phut! they slept in the falling snow, their black painted out to white.

One man got himself a big pre-war fire truck with eighteen gears, engine so high off the ground that a child could stand underneath. He fixed up an asbestos platform with a tiny woodsman's stove on top and bolted the lot under the engine. By fuelling the stove he could keep his truck warm enough to be driven and he started a brisk business in grocery delivery. When anyone heard the clang of the fire bell or saw the great chrome radiator grille pushing towards their block, they ran out, limbs and overcoats, stopping him for milk and potatoes. From a distance, because the engine was so high off the ground, you could see the stove eye burning, glowing down the blanked-out streets and past the forgotten cars.

There was another man had six huskies that he harnessed to a home-made sledge. He was Polish and had come to New York to escape the war. No one was exactly sure how he had sneaked six huskies past Immigration but the story goes that the dogs were puppies and the officer, a born and bred city man, didn't believe they would grow any bigger. Besides, didn't his own wife love her chihuahua?

Around the markets of Orchard Street and Essex Street, everyone knew Raphael and his dogs. He made a living selling fruit-flavoured cheeses, his own secret recipe handed down from an uncle who had worked in the kitchens of the Tsar. If Raphael seemed eccentric, he was no more so than all the others who had been blown off their natural course and were learning new orbits around new suns.

When the snow started to fall, Raphael, under his vegetable

sacks stuffed with dog hair and feathers, remembered a time before he was born, before his father was born, when someone who was still in his blood had travelled over the ice plains and the stilled rivers to fill a sledge with furs. The dogs growled at the snow falling in whispers, snow in flakes, snow in footballs, snow in avalanches, gaining mastery over the most modern city in the world. They too began to remember, and under their paws were the white rocks of the Eskimo, and stunted wind-mad plants, and volcanic sulphurous geysers, and outside, the short-fringed ponies, and other creatures, unseen, howling in the night. They were ready.

All night Raphael worked, hammering, sawing, bending, shaping, oiling, planing, fining, and there was wood, rope, metal and leather, and the dogs fetching in their mouths the things he needed.

By morning they were ready. In the raw dawn of a dead day, along deserted Fifth Avenue, the sound of bells, the sound of dogs barking, a whip in the cracking air, and a cry as old as winter itself. Raphael in his chariot, his hair black as coal, his eyes bright as living coal, spinning the snow under the rails of the sled.

People crowded out to him to get black tea or pea and ham soup from the two gleaming samovars. He sold bagels with his own fruit cheeses. He sold bars of dark chocolate and a patent chest ointment made of peppermint oil. The dogs, shaking the snow from their ruffs, were popular with the children, and bared their gleaming teeth and steaming tongues in greeting.

People called his sled and team 'The Angel Car'. He ran errands for the oldest and the youngest hitched lifts, piled in childish heaps behind the hissing copper cylinders.

New York, city of motion, could not go forward, and so, because it hated to stand still, it went backwards. Went backwards into its past, individual and collective, the past of the place; the Hudson river and the trappers, the Indians and their piebald horses, the Dutch Stuyvesants, trading, building, navigating, dealing. The past of its people, now from so many parts of the globe, but all knowing what it was to struggle, to pioneer. To make the difficulty into the dream.

The snow recast the buildings into mountains. Tiny figures huddled in all of their clothes and all of their bedclothes, padded without sound in the shadow of these mountains. They were hunting food, hunting company, they were bartering what they had for what they wanted.

To defy the silence of the snow people began to sing. The layers-deep of snow baffled the acoustics, so that someone a few streets away from a song, could not hear the notes, but could feel the vibration. The sound of the city singing shook its foundations so seismically that after the snow melted, a number of buildings were found to have lost their tops.

Anyone going about in those days would come upon fires lit on the sidewalks where groups of men and women congregated for warmth away from their swooned apartments. Then somebody else would arrive with a stone jar of Schnapps, and somebody else with a hod of chestnuts and somebody else with a mouth organ, and there was Raphael running up and down with red-hot pitchers, filling the mugs we all carried with us in those days.

I say 'we all' for I was about to be born.

My mother, big with child, had strange longings; she wanted to eat diamonds. This gastronomic extravagance could hardly have been more than a fantasy for all but the very rich and Papa could not afford a Guggenheim bagel. We were not rich, nor were Papa's many friends but some of them were diamond dealers, trading silently, secretively in a huddle of patched-up buildings around Canal Street and the Bowery.

One evening, when I was six months old, pre-born, bouncing my hands and feet off Mama's womb wall, I heard the voices of Papa's business friends, talking quietly in our warm low kitchen. Mama shouldn't have been present at all, but she cared very little for the strict protocol of his Orthodox friends and banged about the kitchen, sometimes openly hostile, sometimes serving towers of blinis tall as the Empire State. She did as she pleased and no one dared to challenge her because she had saved Papa's life and risked her own. They called her Rahab.

Somewhere from deep inside their coats, their jackets, their shirts, their vests, their skin, their bones, the men unfolded felt pouches and spread the contents, glittering. It was not their value that they were discussing with Papa, it was their capacity to stimulate the soul's deeper life. To a Jew, stones have meaning beyond value. The twelve jewels of the High Priest's breastplate were energy not hoard. The stones live.

Mama turned round from her usual awning of aluminium saucepans and saw the diamonds. I saw their light and pressed myself as close as I could to the membrane of my genial prison. The light struck through Mama's belly and fed me.

She stepped forward, picked up a diamond between thumb and finger, and swallowed it.

Then she swallowed another, and another, a voluntary force-feeding into a priceless pâté: Mama's oesophagus larded with light.

Papa's people are a patient people who have known adversity.

They have wept by the waters of Babylon. They have crossed the Red Sea. They have sat in the desert with their camels and their concubines. They have wandered in the wilderness forty years. They have bargained with their God. Yet not even Job in all his affliction had his inheritance eaten by a woman with child. There was some debate about what to do next.

Papa's people are a patient people. It was agreed that Papa would lock the door to our only lavatory on the landing and persuade Mama to use a commode.

A twenty-four-hour watch was rota'd in the kitchen and one of the off-duty men went out to buy surgical gloves.

Mama had no objection. She wanted only to eat the diamonds not to digest them. No one thought about me.

And I did not think, turning in the weightless water, charmed by cut faces of light.

At last it was over, hats off, sleeves rolled up, sweat on their beards, and the much travelled diamonds shining again on their sterilised cloths.

'*a'dank! mazel tov! bo'ruch ha'bo! Schnapps!*'

'What? One missing? *Oy oy oy oy oy! Oy va-avoy! Vai!*'

Castor oil. Enema. Glycerine suppositories. Salt water colon irrigation. Cabbage soup. *Schnell, kroit zup!*

No use. No use at all. I had captured it or it had captured me. After a night of prayer this was revealed to the Elders in a dream. 'We will attend the birth,' they said, at belly level, directly to me, usurper of jewels, infant smuggler of precious stones.

*

At night, when Mama slept and the lights were out and the night was dark, Papa stood over her in his shawl and guiltily lifted her nightdress. He had never seen her naked, not seen the gentle demands of her, the map that she was where he might have travelled.

He put out his hand but he was afraid. Her belly shone.

Still the snow. Pillow feathers of snow. Shook eiderdowns of snow. The snow in sheets on the river. The snow that quilted the park. The city had become a linen department of snow. Snow on snow at Rossetti's diner, the most famous little trat in town. FOOD TASTES BETTER IN ITALIAN. Their little boy used to hand out black olives. We think Mama was heading there on the night she gave birth. The olives tasted of jet.

It was the time of her confinement. A couple of Elders, on rota, sat with Papa in the kitchen, arguing about Sodom and Gomorrah. Mama was no pillar of salt and without looking back she left the apartment by the fire escape. She had her fur-collar coat from the Vienna days and warm boots. She felt well and happy, tired of the encampment of old men, and crazy to eat something bright and hard. I was ready to go anywhere.

Mama walked, thinking of better times when she had listened to Strauss and read Nietzsche. She thought of the café where she had met Papa, where everyone wanted to talk, and hardly noticed until it was too late, what was happening outside.

'Shadows, signs, wonders,' Papa had said, meaning the world. Didn't he admit by now that the shadow had substance enough?

And yet . . . her country, her family, her past seemed to have vanished as easily as Papa said they could. What was real? What was in her hands? Her father had joined the Nazis and had been hung from a hook in his own shop. She had no news of her mother or her brothers. No news of her war-beaten homeland. She was an exile now. She had joined Papa's people after all. How many years had passed, seven, eight, nine? What did it matter? Nowhere was real now but this twelve and a half by two and a half mile island.

She thought she was walking towards the lights but her thoughts had overrun her and she had lost her way. The snowed city was a white maze. Where was she? She had come down Christopher Street and was at the Hudson river. She saw the great doors of the Cunard Building. First Class. Cabin Class. She could hear rough noises from the Anchor Café where the sailors met and far out were the fog lamps of a trader ship passing through the Narrows.

Over the slow water, skimming towards her, a stellated brightness, a cast jewel, and another and another fast behind. Was it from the ship? She strained her eyes, she tried to make a telescope of her retina, to track the quick flashes as they moved. When she was little, her father had taken her to the sea and made flat stones skip over the tops of the waves. Each one, he had said, flew on to another country, rested at last at a shore beyond the sea. She fancied that these hard bright things were souls like her. Souls joining the bodies that had gone ahead of them, in rags, in sorrow, in haste, unwilling, dead bodies over the sea, leaving their souls behind.

The world had heaved up. Much had been left behind.

Perhaps this was her chance. Would her soul return? She put her hands down over her belly and felt me there. In a second of shock she realised she was going into labour. How cold it was.

How dark. She saw the Morse uncoded light once more and fainted.

It was Raphael who found her.

Raphael, ears keen as his dogs', had been delivering cigarettes to the Anchor Café. As he came out of the smoky light into the unfiltered darkness, he heard someone calling him . . . 'Raphael! Raphael!'

'Here I am, Lord,' he said, remembering the story of Samuel.

Who called him? My mother was unconscious.

He drove his sled over to the rail and although he was a tiny man he picked up Mama and me and laid her in the sacks on the sled. We set off, Raphael wondering wildly what to do with the unknown woman and her almost-child. He was afraid of hospitals.

Along Fifth Avenue, past the grand houses lit with candles, in an heroic effort to save electricity. When Raphael had first come to New York he used to stand opposite Mrs Vanderbilt's on the corner of 51st and marvel at her four red roses, fresh each day, in the window of her huge library. Now they were building the Rockefeller Center on the site. Raphael admired the progress but missed the roses.

Not there. Not there. The grandees wouldn't take them in, the improbable duo on their snow-sped sledge. The dogs ran faster and faster, not driven, leading, hoping for a sign, a place to stop. There was no one out on the streets.

And Papa?

He began to call. He called from the Creation. He called from the flocks of Abraham. He called from Jacob's wiliness. He called out of Pharaoh's dream. He called with the rod of Moses. He called with the voice of the prophets he called with the ecstasy of David. He called up the light that was in him and Raphael heard it. 'Raphael, Raphael!' Again 'Raphael, Raphael!'

The dogs slithered to a stop, turned, obeyed the frequency, higher than 30 megahertz, and ran forwards.

The Temple Emanu-el. Papa was on the steps. As the sledge curved to a halt there was a cry from behind.

I was born.

A life for a life. She had saved him. Now he had saved us. Mama never believed that, of course not. That Papa with his shawl, his boxes, his stones, his books, his mutterings, his sleepless years, could pierce events and alter them, that was not science. Not common sense. She thanked chance and Raphael, and only once did she look at Papa as though she might, perhaps, believe him. He said, 'I was able to find you because you were radiant. That night the light in you was strong.'

She thought of the stellated brightness spinning towards her and what had she fancied about it being her soul?

She looked at him, and whether or not she believed him, from that time a debt was paid. They had rescued each other. It was the end of their marriage though we continued under the same roof, the three of us until 1959, when I was twelve.

Whether or not she believed him she named me Stella after her star. Papa named me Sarah, after the wife of Abraham who gave birth to a child when she was ninety-three. 'For with God,' Papa said, 'nothing is impossible.'

You will want to know about the diamond.

When it was discovered that I had been born, every diamond

92

dealer on Canal St came to visit me. The placenta was thoroughly examined before Mama ate it as was the custom among her Bavarian ancestors. She had it fried with onions in one of the aluminium saucepans. That was one, at least, that Papa would not use again.

A doctor came, and the man who rigged the lights for Times Square. In the old days, before neon, Times Square was incandescent, and it was some of these incandescent wands of power that Duke brought with him.

The doctor positioned me. The diamond dealers crowded round. Signora Rossetti, from Mama's favourite diner, had brought squid and ciabatta to hand round. This was a party, a fairground, a miracle, the world's first pre-mortem.

Duke switched on his lights bright as Creation, and I hung there, turning, turning in my harness, my skin a pale transparent shawl over my new made bones.

The diamond was at the base of my spine by the sacroiliac joint.

Oy oy oy, nu?

Well?

The doctor said that the diamond could not be mined without crippling me. No one wanted to do that even if I had been born of a shikseh.

Papa shrugged. 'OK, OK, let's talk *tachles*.'

The men sat down to business, and at last agreed to raise a collection for the lost diamond, so that its rightful owner need not lose more than face. Would that settle it?

Yes and no.

Even today the man's son still follows me wherever I go, waiting for the moment when he can claim his family property. When

I die I shall go to the Jewish mortuary and have my birthright surgically removed.

I have left the diamond to the Glinerts in my Will.

'What kind of a story is that?' said Jove.

TEN OF SWORDS

August 14 1940. Rome, Italy. Sun in Leo.

Jove, born Giovanni Baptista Rossetti, a lion cub of goatish parents who emigrated to New York City in 1942.

Signora Rossetti remade herself from peasant into one of Pasta's Famous Faces. In 1942 she had sunk her small savings into a delicatessen and trattoria and built up the business into an export empire and restaurant franchise. Her shrewd success had been based on more than olive oil and durum wheat. She was something of a back-kitchen psychologist.

Signora Rossetti had realised that her American-speaking customers would learn only two words of Italian: 'Spaghetti' and 'Quanto?' Faced with a foreign language they ordered by numbers. 'I'll take an eighteen.' To save them further trouble Signora Rossetti dispensed with language altogether. Her menu was a list of numbers, out of series, with further numbers in dollars, lire and sterling, to reassure the cost-conscious monoglot looking for an authentic foreign experience. So homely and honest and genuine seemed Signora Rossetti that British and American customers formed long queues outside the front door. They did not realise that the Italians and the Irish went around the back with a *'Ciao Mama bella bella'* and took any table they liked.

No. 18, the most popular item on the menu, a secret recipe hamburger made with garlic and herbs. Although it was the only hamburger on the menu, her front door diners seemed to find it by instinct. 'I'll take an eighteen.' When they did not, Mama served it to them anyway . . .

'Diciotto . . .'

Soon, the people who queued at the front door came to believe that *diciotto* was Italian for hamburger and Signora Rossetti was able to sell a franchise of Diciotto Houses all over America. There, anyone could buy diciotto and fries on a warm bed of spaghetti topped with a sesame-seed bun.

Of course, when the Sixties came, and America was looking outwards again, everyone spoke Italian and Signora Rossetti was rumbled. By then, who cared? Signora Rossetti, fat and famous, wrote a ribbon at the top of her syndicated menus: FOOD TASTES BETTER IN ITALIAN.

At least that was the story as Jove told it to me.

'Story of my life, Alice?' he said. 'The bright boy who loves and hates America. Loves it because it has given him everything. Hates it because it has given him everything. The ambivalence of the immigrant everywhere.'

Endlessly he talked of returning to Italy and never returned and lost in him were the warm slow days, the smell of ripening tomatoes, the dogs yapping out on the terrace, his father's country vineyard where the hills were steep with donkeys.

Sometimes the lost places overtook him and he started shouting about crazy progress and crazy life and why were the best brains in their field voluntarily working harder than in the bad days of bought slaves in the cotton field?

He said, 'If I am master of my life why do I feel so out of control?'

Jove. He had been among the first of the younger physicists to criticise The Standard Model; the comprehensive theory of matter that seems to fit with so much of the experimental data. Jove called it 'The Flying Tarpaulin'; big, ugly, useful, covers what you want and ignores gravity. The attraction of the Model is that it recognises the symmetries of the three fundamental forces, weak force, strong force, electromagnetic force. Difficulties begin when these three separate forces are arbitrarily welded together.

His wife, his mistress, met.

In the 1970s Jove was working on his GUTs: Grand Unified Theories that sought to unite the strong, weak, and electromagnetic quanta in a sympathetic symmetry that would include gravity and overturn the bolt-it-together-somehow methods of The Standard Model.

GUTs had their heart in the right place; they wanted to recognise the true relationship between the three fundamental forces. Now, more than ever, crossing into the twenty-first century, our place in the universe and the place of the universe in us, is proving to be one of active relationship. This is more than a scientist's credo. The separateness of our lives is a sham. Physics, mathematics, music, painting, my politics, my love for you, my work, the star-dust of my body, the spirit that impels it, clocks diurnal, time perpetual, the roll, rough, tender, swamping, liberating, breathing, moving, thinking nature, human nature and the cosmos are patterned together.

Symmetry. Beauty. Perhaps it seems surprising that physicists seek beauty but in fact they have no choice. As yet there has not been an exception to the rule that the demonstrable solution to any problem will turn out to be an aesthetic solution.

'The tougher the problem the more beautiful the solution,' said Jove, smiling at me, frowning at my mathematics.

Later, in bed, inside me, 'The short and organised equations of physics are as beautiful and surprising as the natural forces they interpret.'

Jove had a way of being in the right place at the right time. As enthusiasm for GUTs weakened (negative experimental data), he hauled himself up through the body of science on a Superstring.

According to the theory, any particle, sufficiently magnified, will be seen not as a solid fixed point but as a tiny vibrating string. Matter will be composed of these vibrations. The universe itself would be symphonic.

If this seems strange, it is stranger that the image of the universe as a musical instrument, vibrating divine harmonies, was a commonplace of Renaissance thought. Robert Fludd's *Utriusque Cosmi Historia* (1617–19) has a diagram of the tunings and harmonies of this instrument, according to the heavenly spheres. 'As above, so below' may prove to be more than a quaint alchemical axiom. Following the Superstring theory, the symmetry we observe in our universe is only a remnant of the symmetry to be observed in perfect ten-dimensional space.

'Jove only works on Superstrings because it reminds him of spaghetti,' said Signora Rossetti.

'Mama!' screamed Jove, forgetting that he was grown up, distinguished, important, respected and nearly bald.

Mama had long since packed up and bought a villa in Positano and an apartment in Rome. She wanted Jove to go home and be an Italian again. Jove, for all his dreams of basil plants on a sunny window-sill, had New York in his belly. New York was where he belonged. He fought with his Roman Mama, but liked her nickname for him as King of the Gods. He could not bring himself to disbelieve it quite, nor could he quite forget that his real name was Giovanni, as in *Don Giovanni*, his favourite opera. Mozart 1787.

He said, 'Who are the world's most famous seducers?'
1) Lothario. A fiction character who first appeared on stage in 1703.
2) Casanova. A fact/fiction. Born in 1725. The man for whom chocolate and mussels were aphrodisiac, and a half lemon (properly inserted) contraceptive.
3) Don Juan/Giovanni. A fiction/fact. Nobody knows whether or not he was real. Everybody knows that this unsheathed-sword-of-a-lifetime was dragged down to Hell for his sins.

'*Purché porti la gonnella, Voi sapete quel che fa.*'

'If she wears a petticoat you know what he does,' sang Jove in the opera chamber of his shower.

Jove/Giovanni, a man with two reputations he wanted to protect: his primacy and his potency. A mistress was as necessary to
him as an atom smasher. He had a joke about it.

What's the difference between a mistress and an atom smasher?

An atom smasher will only cost you $12 billion.

What's the difference between an atom smasher and a mistress?

An atom smasher knows when to stop.

Our affair, like every other, was conducted inside a vas hermeticum: a sealed vessel, shut off from the world, to boil and cool
according to its own laws.

What did we hope for, heating and re-heating ourselves to
absurd temperatures? As matter heats up it is subject to demonstrable change. Boiling in our vessel, our water molecules would
begin to break down, stripping us back to elemental hydrogen and
oxygen gases. Would this help us to see ourselves as we really
are?

Heated further, our atomic structure would be ripped apart. He
and she as plasma again, the most common state of matter in the
universe. Would this bring us closer together?

At about a billion degrees K, give or take a furnace or two, he
and she might begin to counterfeit the interior of a neutron star
and could rapidly be heated further into sub-atomic particles. You
be a quark and I'll be a lepton.

If we had the courage to cook ourselves to a quadrillion
degrees, the splitting, the dividing, the ripping, the hurting, will be
over. At this temperature, the weak force and the electromagnetic
force are united. A little hotter, and the electroweak and the strong
force move together as GUT symmetries appear.

And at last? When gravity and GUTs unite? Listen: one plays

the lute and another the harp. The strings are vibrating and from the music of the spheres a perfect universe is formed. Lover and beloved pass into one another identified by sound.

'And behold I saw a new heaven and a new earth.'

Grandmother reading from the Bible to a child who hardly understood the words but felt strange intimations of grandeur.

Jove and I walking in Vermont among the whirling profligacy of leaves. Under the red, under the orange, red in our pockets, orange in haloes at our head, veins of gold on the ivory-find of each other's bodies.

The sceptical world knee-deep in yods of falling fire.

And after symmetries of autumn, symmetries of austerity. Bare winter's thin beauty, rib and spine. The back of him sharp-boned, my hands leaf-broad covering him, patterning him. Us making love on the leaf-shed in the cold of the year.

Walk with me. Walk time in its skeleton. Walk the white curve of Adam's rib. White, that absorbs the minimum, reflects the maximum of light rays, ecstasy of light at the dead of the year.

Walk with me. Walk the ancient history of his body, recorded in quasars, erupted in light. Kiss him and I kiss the full of him and the dust of him. Touch him where he is firm and my hand passes through into empty space. Love him and I love this man, this body. Love him and I love star-dust and light.

Walk with me. Walk the 6,000,000,000,000 miles of travelled light, single year's journey of illumination, ship miles under the glowing keel. In the long frost the sky brightens and the rim of the earth is pierced by sharp stars. After the leaf-fall the star-fall, the winter shedding of too much light. Walk the seen and unseen. What can be rendered visible and what cannot.

The wind up at dusk and the leaves in squalls and the birds flying into the wind-backed leaves so that in the lost light I could not say where the leaves stopped and the birds began. I try to distinguish but at crucial moments the space between carefully separated objects collapses and I too am whirled up against my will into the dervish of matter. The difficulty is that every firm step I win out of chaos is a firm step towards . . . more chaos. I throw a rope bridge, haul myself across the gap, and huddled on a little outcrop, safe for now, observe the view. What is the view? Another gap, another stretch of water.

The wind at dusk. We were to be the lightest of things, he and I, lifting each other up above the heaviness of life. It was because we knew that gravity is always part of the equation that we tried to defeat it. Lighter than light in the atmosphere of our love.

It was a volatile experiment, soon snared by the ordinariness we set out to resist. Our alchemical transformations, like those of the alchemists before us, became more and more weighed down by the baseness of normal life. Lies, secrets, silences, common currency of deceit.

Say alchemy to most people and they will say, 'Turn metal into gold.' Yet what Paracelsus and the alchemists wanted was to make themselves the living gold. The treasure without moth or rust, spirit (*pneuma*) unalloyed.

Say theoretical physics to most people five hundred years from now and perhaps they will say, 'Bombs and destruction.' How to explain that what we saw, briefly, dimly, was a new heaven and a new earth?

Is crassness bound to win? To live differently, to love differently, to think differently, or to try to. Is the danger of beauty so great that it is better to live without it (The Standard Model)? Or to fall into her arms fire to fire? There is no discovery without risk and what you risk reveals what you value. Inside the horror of Nagasaki and Hiroshima lies the beauty of Einstein's $E = MC^2$.

A man slow of speech and gentle of person. What patterns do the numbers make, breaking and beginning in the waters of his spirit?

And you? Now that I have discovered you? Beautiful, dangerous, unleashed. Still I try to hold you, knowing that your body is faced with knives.

When Jove began to notice me I was puppy-dog glad. Like dogs everywhere I was assured that my man was the best man and love is enough.

'Come out for a walk?'

Woof.

'Like some dinner?'

Woof.

'Sit on my knee.'

Woof.

I resisted him as all abandoned strays do a new home; for at least two days. Even while I was mouthing 'no' my heart was yapping 'yes'.

It had been the same with my father. His interest in me pendulumed from hot intensity to cool indifference. Weeks together would be followed by months apart. Then he would woo me again and each time I was determined to resist. He knew that. He waited. So did Jove.

I thought he made me fully human. I did not think of us as one man and his dog.

When Jove clipped me to him he widened his view. With a dog you can go places you cannot go alone. At his side I was access and envy (What a showpiece. Where did you find her?). At my side he was young and sexy (Will you marry him?). He told me he and his wife were getting a divorce. If I had turned into a dog he had always been a dark horse.

When I asked him for explanations he said, 'I need time.'

Time.

Newton visualised time as an arrow flying towards its target. Einstein understood time as a river, moving forward, forceful, directed, but also bowed, curved, sometimes subterranean, not ending but pouring itself into a greater sea. A river cannot flow against its current, but it can flow in circles; its eddies and whirlpools regularly break up its strong press forward. The riverrun is maverick, there is a high chance of cross-current, a snag of time that returns us without warning to a place we thought we had sailed through long since.

Anyone to whom this happens clings faithfully to the clock; the hour will pass, we will certainly move on. Then we find the clock is neither raft nor lifebelt. The horological illusion of progress sinks. The past comes with us, like a drag-net of fishes. We tow it down river, people and things, emotions, time's inhabitants, not left on shore way back, but still swimming close by.

A kick in the current twists us round, and suddenly we are caught in the net we made, the accumulations of a lifetime just under the surface. What were those stories about townships at the bottom of a river? Lost kingdoms tantalisingly visible when the water was calm? It is well-known that mermaids flash through the dark sea to swim like salmon against the river.

The unconscious, it seems, will not let go of its hoard. The past comes with us and occasionally kidnaps the present, so that the distinctions we depend on for safety, for sanity, disappear. Past. Present. Future. When this happens we are no longer sure who we are, or perhaps we can no longer pretend to be sure who we are.

If time is a river then we shall all meet death by water.

MISSING PRESUMED DEAD

A yacht sailing off Capri was last sighted on Sunday June 16 at 18:00 hours. The boat was in difficulties. Severe storms prevented rescue attempts for 24 hours. It is thought that the boat could be drifting at sea.

We had planned a sailing holiday together, Jove and I. Three weeks of salty confinement on the flashing seas. I wanted to be shut away with him, the certainty of he and I in our precarious world, the world itself, nothing but a navigable sea.

On a boat there is no escape. I wanted no escape. I had been annexed by Jove. What had begun as a comity of sovereign states had ended in invasion. He had invaded me but who was arguing over the boundaries? I hardly cared that sharing had come to be spelled capture. Intellectually I was emancipated. Emotionally I still lived in a seraglio. I had been waiting for my prince to come.

I had found relief with Jove and did not question it. Relief from the burden of myself. Here was a recognised pattern with room in it for my piece. My gaps and angles now fitted somewhere. I was joined up, part of a whole not awkward, standing out. The cloak of invisibility conferred by coupledom meant that I was no longer Alice but Alice and Jove. There were two of us to reckon with. Two names on the invitation.

And then there were three.

His wife, his mistress, met.

PAGE OF CUPS

I met Stella at the Algonquin Hotel. The Algonquin Hotel; Dorothy Parker, James Thurber, *The New Yorker*, my father in 1957. He had stayed there because it seemed so English and when he brought me to New York for the first time as a child our reservations were at the Algonquin Hotel.

He had booked his old room and even packed a tie he used to wear in those days. Red silk with little white polka dots, he never would say who had given it to him.

'Never tell all thy love.'

Like my grandmother he kept secrets the way other people keep fish. They were a hobby, a fascination, his underwater collection of the rare and the strange. Occasionally something would float up to the surface, unexpected, unexplained.

Mother said: 'Why didn't you tell me?'

Father said: 'There was nothing to tell.'

I am my father's daughter.

She and I would be approaching the place from opposite ends of town. I imagined her, angry, confident, ready to match me and beat me at my own game. This was the big fight and Jove the prize. When I told him she had written to me he had decided to visit friends for the weekend.

I had her letter in my pocket. The careful handwriting. The instruction to obey. 'I will meet you on Wednesday the 12th at 6:30 p.m. in the bar at the Algonquin Hotel.'

Why had she chosen here?

Here it was.

Five minutes to spare. The cruelty of time.

I had dressed as a warrior: black from cleavage to insoles, hair down, fat hoops of gold in my ears, war-paint make-up. I had a twenty-year advantage over my opponent and I intended to use every month of it.

She would be greying, she would be lined, she would be over-weight, she would be clothes-careless. She would be poetically besocked and sandalled, her eyes behind glass, like museum exhibits. I could see her, hair and flesh escaping, hope trapped inside. I would drain her to the sump.

No sign of her. The bar was a chessboard of couples manoeuvring Martinis, and waiters high-carrying chrome trays. I moved in black knight right angles across and cross the lines but apart from a few appreciative businessmen there was no one who seemed interested in me.

Of course she had not come. Of course she would not come. It had been a nerve war and I had won. I noticed I had a terrible pain in my neck. I ordered a drink and collapsed under a potted palm.

'May I sit here?'

'Please do. You must be English.'

'Why?'

'Too polite to be an American.'

'Aren't Americans polite?'

'Only if you pay them enough.'

'The British aren't polite no matter how much you pay them.'

'Then you and I must be refugees.'

'I suppose I am. My father used to come here. He loved New York. He said it was the only place in the world where a man could be himself while working his shirt off to become somebody else.'

'And did he?'

'What?'

'Become somebody else.'

'Yes. Yes he did.'

We were quiet. She was looking towards the door. I looked at her. She was slim, wired, a greyhound body, half bent forward now, shape of her back muscles contouring her shirt, white, starched, expensive. Her left arm looked like the front window of Tiffany's. I was not sure how a woman could wear so much silver and sit without a lean.

Her hair was dark red, dogwood red, leather red with a suppleness to it that is part gift, part effort. I guessed that the look of hers was as artful as it was artless.

'Are you waiting for someone?' I said.

'I was.' She looked at her watch. 'Are you staying here?'

'No. I live in New York. I work at the Institute for Advanced Studies. I came here to meet . . .'

To meet: to come face to face with. To become acquainted with. To be introduced. To find. To experience. To receive. To await the arrival of. To encounter. To encounter in conflict.

'I came here to meet . . .'

There was a wind in the room that tore the drink out of the drinkers, that scattered the bar bottles like bottle tops, that levitated the furniture and smashed it into the tranced wall. Waiters and waited on blew in rags out of the door. There was nothing left in the room but she and me, she and me hypnotised by each other, unable to speak because of the wind.

She gathered her things and together we left the destroyed room. I had to follow her as she twisted the pavements under her feet. I lost sense of where we were. The grid had buckled. The city was a bent alley and she was the better rat.

At last we arrived at a small diner in a beaten-up part of town. She swung inside and we sat at a menacingly nice checked-cloth table with two carnations and a few rods of grissini. A boy came out with a carafe of red wine and a bowl of olives. He handed us the menus as if this was just an ordinary dinner in an ordinary day. I had fallen into the hands of the Borgias and now they wanted me to eat.

I looked at the menu. FOOD TASTES BETTER IN ITALIAN.

'This is where I met him,' she said. 'In 1947 on the day that I was born . . .'

★

The little boy had been asleep and through his dreams came a sleigh piled with furs and followed on foot by a band of wild dark men, huddled hurrying, talking in a language he did not understand. He heard barking and crying and from below the protesting water being drawn along the frozen pipes and into the geyser. He woke up and ran downstairs. The chairs and tables had been pushed back against the walls and the double doors onto the street were open. Through the blue curtain of cold, into the orange lights, six wolves drew a sledge. The leading pair pulled up two inches from his chest and level with it. One of the wolves licked his face with its brown-pink parma ham tongue. Now he would be eaten.

'Mama! Mama! Mama! Il lupo mi mangierá!'

'Eccola, Romulo,' said Signora Rossetti, and the little boy was hoisted over the grinning dogs and told how Romulus and Remus, the abandoned twins, had been suckled by a she-wolf and thus saved to found the great city of Rome.

Not wishing to be outdone, the Elders all began to tell stories at once of Hebrew heroes and animal help: Abraham's ram, Balaam's ass, Jacob's lion, Samson's bees. Job's entire menagerie, including the horse that danced and crieth among the trumpets 'Aha!'

'And our Saviour himself,' said Signora Rossetti, whose contribution was met with a generally icy stare colder than the air outside.

But this was no night to pick quarrels and over polenta and kirsch it was agreed that Jesus could be included because he was Jewish and because he had been assisted at birth by donkeys, sheep and dogs.

The little boy had never seen a baby pink as a wolf's tongue.

★

As she told the story she forgot about me. I had begun as an adversary, become an audience, and now seemed only a footlight. The stage was hers and if she was performing for anyone it was herself.

A very good performer she was; breaking into Yiddish, into Italian, into German, accenting and gesturing, turning now into a claque of elderly Jews, now into a frightened small boy. I had to let go of my detachment, my resentment. When she imitated the horse that crieth among the trumpets 'Aha!', I was back with Grandmother again, back with the weekly visits and the preposterous slippers, the huge full-length apron, its pocket stuffed with Polo mints and a battered Bible.

Perhaps it was the seriousness of our business that pushed us both into laughter, extremes of emotion so easily tumbling into their opposites. Yet there was relief for us to find a human face behind the monster mask; the monster wife, the monster mistress, and what about the monster man?

'He was a flirt even then,' said Stella. 'He flirted with Mama who had a weakness for dark hair and dark eyes, even in a seven-year-old boy.'

'But Jove is younger than you.'

'Did he tell you that?'

'You were born in 1940. He was born in 1947.'

'The other way round.'

And she told me how she and her mother had visited the diner once a week, on a Saturday, for the next eleven years. It had to be Saturday. The Jewish Shabbat. Papa's ecstasy. Mama's defiance. Her daughter was not Jewish. Jewishness is continued through the female line. Mama would not have her daughter given up to Papa's passion.

Mother and daughter, secular, apart. Papa beckoning the child in unwatched moments, taking her into his secret room, showing her symbols and precious stones. She had navigated her parents' hostile waters with a child's discretion, learning to keep from one the confessions of the other. Learning to hide love.

When she was eleven, Papa died. Within three months Mother in a little black suit, child in a black warm coat, took ship to Hamburg and re-settled in Berlin. The books and the bookshop had been sold and the secret room was empty.

While she was talking I wondered why Jove wanted me. I had come out dressed to kill and I was the one being murdered. My self-esteem is a jigsaw I cannot complete. I get one part of the picture and the rest lies in pieces. I suspect that there is no picture, only fragments. Other people seem to glue it together somehow and not to worry that they have been using pieces from several different boxes. So what is the answer? Is identity a deceit, a make-shift, and should we hurry to make any pattern we can? Or is there a coherence, perhaps a beauty, if it were possible to find it? I would like to convince myself about myself but I cannot. The best there is are days when the jigsaw assumes its own meaning and I no longer care what picture is emerging. By that I mean I am unfrightened by the unexpected. If there is beauty it will surprise me. Of all things it cannot be calculated. I said I suspect that there is no picture. I should have said that whatever the picture is, it will not be the one on the box.

ME: I am sorry.

SHE: This isn't the first time.

ME: I know that.

SHE: They always do.

ME: I thought I might be the one.

SHE: They always do.

ME: You could leave him.

SHE: To you?

ME: To himself.

SHE: Simple in books.

ME: Not in your books.

SHE: Words, words, he says.

ME: Safety in numbers.

SHE: Even the hairs of your head are numbered . . .

ME: What number am I?

SHE: Five.

ME: That's lucky.

SHE: Said to ward off the Evil Eye.

ME: I thought that was you.

SHE: Little round glasses?

ME: Socks and sandals.

SHE: Fat, beery.

ME: Out of touch.

SHE: Give me your hand.

ME: What?

SHE: I'll read it for you.

ME: What do you see?

SHE: Beauty and fear.

ME: You aren't looking.

SHE: I used to say that to Papa.

ME: What did he say?

SHE: What you see is not what you think you see.

ME: Sound science.

SHE: Doesn't that depend on the scientist?

ME: I wouldn't depend on the scientist . . .

SHE: If I were you?

ME: It isn't a warning.

SHE: A threat?

ME: Do I look like a threat?

SHE: You look exactly like the previous four threats.

ME: What are you going to do?

SHE: What would you like me to do?

★

It was what Jove had said a few months ago when he had been holding my wrist, too tightly, across a restaurant table. She was still holding my hand and what I did was outside of anything I had imagined I would do.

I leaned across the narrow table and kissed her.

SHE: Women as well?

ME: No.

Cowardice bedshares with arrogance. I was afraid and I wanted to bluff my way out. The kiss was a smoke bomb to cause confusion and distract attention. I thought she might slap me. I thought she would rush away. In fact she did nothing. Asked her question and did nothing. I started to re-eat my cold pasta. I would have been glad to climb into the plate and cover myself in clam sauce.

ME: I'm working on antiquarks.

SHE:

ME: They are the antiparticles corresponding to the quarks.

SHE:

ME: They haven't been discovered yet.

SHE:

ME: That makes them quite difficult to work on.

SHE:

(Say something please say something.)

★

ME: Did you know I was born on a tug-boat in the River Mersey?

SHE:

ME: My father wanted to call me Mersey but my mother wouldn't let him.
My real name is Alluvia. I shortened it to Alice.

SHE: Alluvia?

ME: That which is deposited by the river.

SHE: Shall I call you Moses?

ME: If I grow a beard.

SHE: Jove calls you Rivelleto.

ME: Little River?

SHE: I call him a mamzer.

ME: Mamzer?

SHE: Yiddish. Look it up under Bastard.

ME: I know.

SHE: Come on.

Walk with me. Walk the broken past, named and not. Walk the splintered plank, chaos on both sides, walk the discovered and what cannot be discovered. Walk the uneasy peace we share.

Walk with me, through the night, the night air, the breathing particles of other lives. Breathe in, breathe out, steady now, not too fast on gassed lungs. I did not mean my words to poison you.

Walk with me, walk it off, the excess fat of misery and fear. Too much to carry around the heart. Walk free.

She had a long stride though I was taller. Soon we were at the Battery.

Valet de Coupe. A youth stares anxiously into an elaborate cup whose contents are concealed. There may be no contents. Nevertheless he holds onto the cup. Carrying it with him as he walks.

Page of Cups. Young hopeful of the Tarot deck. My identity card.

When Stella kissed me I remember thinking, 'This is not allowed.' I was glad of the fog and the dark because I knew that if anyone saw us, the totality of our lives; history, complexity, nationality, intelligence, age, achievement, status, would be shrunk up to the assumptions of our kiss. Whoever saw us would say, 'There's a couple of . . .', and this kiss, tentative, ambivalent, would become a lock and key.

I had seen it happen to others. I did not want it to happen to me.

At the same time I realised the absurdity of pinning anything onto a kiss.

At the same time I realised that I would like to do much more kissing if it were not so complicated.

So complicated. My first serious emotion was for a married man. My first experience of authentic desire was with a married woman.

You see, I did want to kiss her. That was what surprised me most of all.

'I see why he likes you,' said Stella, examining my neck with her fingers.

'Is that why you're doing it?'

'I don't know what I'm doing.'

I would argue with that.

She took me home, didn't put on any lights, took off her clothes and had me lie down beside her on what seemed to be a very narrow bed. I wanted to touch her. The reflecting image of a woman with a woman is seductive. I enjoyed looking at her in a way that was forbidden to me, this self on self, self as desirer and desired, had a frankness to it I had not been invited to discover. Desiring her I felt my own desirability. It was an act of power but not power over her. I was my own conquest.

Her breasts as my breasts, her mouth as my mouth, were more than Narcissus hypnotised by his own likeness. Everybody knows how the story changes when he disturbs the water. I did disturb the water and the perfect picture broke. You see, I could have rested there beside her, perhaps forever, it felt like forever, a mirror confusion of bodies and sighs, undifferentiated, she in me, me in she and no longer exhausted by someone else's shape over mine. And I had not expected such intense physical pleasure.

Why then did I trouble the surface?

It was not myself I fell in love with it was her.

Deeper now where the water is not clear. What patterns do the numbers make? One plus one is not necessarily two. I do the sum and the answer is an incipient third. Three pairs of two: Jove and

Stella, Jove and Alice, Alice and Stella, and under the surface of each the head of the other.

I want to feel but with feeling comes pain. I could advise myself to keep out of complications and I won't pretend that I have had no choice in any of this. I have noticed that choices seem to be made in advance of what is chosen. The time gap in between the determining will and the determined event is a handy excuse to deny causality. In space-time there is always a lag between prediction and response (synchronicity is a higher dimension phenomenon where the rules of space-time do not apply), sometimes of seconds, sometimes of years, but we programme events far more than we like to think. I do not say this is conscious, usually it is not, and there lies the difficulty. I have seen my father pushing the world, he quite unaware of what was pushing him. He did not believe in the unconscious, except as a soup of fantasy and half-memories that entertained his sleep. To suggest, as I did, that the mind is a self-regulating system, where consciousness and unconsciousness work as load-balancing pulleys, roused anger enough to make me think I had touched something relevant. I continued my reading: Paracelsus, Jung, Einstein, Freud, Capra, and although I still know nothing, I am no longer a disciple of Fate.

Fate. A spin on the Wheel of Fortune and out I tumbled at Jove's feet. Another dizzy round, and there is Stella waiting to help me off. But who is turning the wheel? Honest Guv' I had both hands tied behind my back.

My father used to tell me I had an octopus-complex. 'Must you try and do eight things at once?' I used to imagine that there was an octopus, hooded, ancient, floating in the limp waters of my body, reaching out, dark and blind, using its tentacles to probe what stood outside it. Analogies fail, but I am capable of behaving like an eight-armed cephalopod while protesting the innocence of my two hands on the table.

I wear a white coat, tie my hair back and assume the proper attitude to what I call my life. I will examine it, but underneath the dark things stir. What would happen if I came face to face with what I am? I think it is happening but because I do not recognise myself I say it is somebody else; him, her, them, who are responsible. Responsible for my terror. Every piece of furniture in the room has been destroyed.

I woke up in the dazed apartment. Next to me on the massacred bed, the order and beauty of her body. On the table beside, an amputated lamp. Across the room was a Snow Queen's mirror, its pieces scatters of despair. I crept from beneath the scissored blankets to the bathroom. The white and chrome was a shrine to Chanel. A place for everything, everything in its place. Peace.

I sniffed the bottles. Here were the secrets of irresistible skin and salt smells of pearl and oyster. Lemon, brine, seaweed, sandalwood, musk, bitter rock-rose, frankincense and myrrh. Not here the floral notes of the high-octave female. I admire the soprano singer but not the soprano speaker. High voices like high heels are a put-on. Unfortunately only the shoes get kicked off at night.

Did I say that? No she did. I sometimes think my personality is a troopship's atoll; invade me.

Tell the story as it happened.

Alluvia: the deposits collected and jetted by the river.

We cooked breakfast in the remains of the frying pan and ate our food standing up, looking out of the window over to the park.

'Every day with Papa,' she said. 'Through the park to Amsterdam Avenue. When I look out of this window I am looking back into the past. It's one of those wormholes you people talk about, a membrane between now and then. A tunnel of energy. I work here, at this window, pulling in the past like Rapunzel's hair.'

I was going to say that wormholes are only a theoretical possibility. But Stella wasn't listening to me.

'How do you think I got the Jackson Pollock?'

(Did she mean the big canvas of violent colour hung in a crude wood frame?)

I said, 'Tell me.'

Central Park. New York. Papa walking every morning in one direction, Miss Peggy Guggenheim being driven every morning in the other direction. Papa was a handsome man and took off his hat to the great lady, shrewd as she was rich, patron of painters, collector of fortunes and spender of them.

Papa may have been in love with her as some people love movie stars and he liked to talk about her to the street sweepers and garbage collectors who know everything, living as they do, in the intimacy of human leftovers.

One of these men, Macy, thin as a shovel, tough as a pick, collected modern art. That is, when his day's work was done he went down to Washington Square, where any number of artists had studios round about and offered to do odd jobs in return for a little drawing or a bit of paint. There was always plumbing to fix, roofs to patch, and he had become a familiar figure with his bag of tools in one hand and his portfolio case in the other. He was the one who took Papa to meet Jackson Pollock.

'Cans of the stuff,' whispered Macy, as Pollock threw paint over his floor-pinned canvas and rolled himself over it from end to end. Papa thought of the ecstasy of David who danced before the Lord.

'Are they expensive?'

'Hell no,' said Macy. 'Just pay him for the paint.'

1947. The year I was born and the year that strange Wyoming-born Pollock exhibited his Action Paintings in New York. Papa took me to the opening and it was no disadvantage that my eyes could not yet focus. In his long black coat and deep hat he carried my head over the crowds, little body dangling beneath. We were at a Shabbat of rioting light. When Pollock was killed in a car crash in 1956 he was famous.

Mama wanted Papa to sell the painting, still rolled up, never framed, but he refused, and kept it from her. When I came back to New York in 1970, it was with the rest of his property, left to me, in the fading old offices of his attorney. We unrolled it together and even the dust shone.

'You know, it isn't insured. I can't afford the premiums.'

She smiled. 'Jove wouldn't let me hang it until he found out what it was worth and then when he found out what it is worth he said we couldn't possibly hang it.'

Jove. The name hung between us.

SHE: Are you in love with him?

ME: Yes. No. Am I?

SHE: I'm not your mother although he is old enough to be your father.

ME: I thought you and he had an arrangement.

SHE: We do. He arranges things and tells me later.

ME: I don't understand.

SHE: You don't know him.

ME: Don't I?

SHE: A man is more than his penis. Not much more but something.

ME: Have I missed the something?

SHE: I have been married to him for twenty-four years.

ME: Then it must be quite a something.

SHE: I deserved that.

ME: Do you want me to go away?

SHE: No. No, actually I want you to stay.

ME: Who with?

SHE: Sometimes I wonder which is which. Where I begin. Where he ends.

ME: You love him.

SHE: Too simple.

ME: About last night . . .

SHE: Is it in the past already?

ME: I didn't mean that.

SHE: We were talking about Jove.

ME: Tell me.

When Mama and I left for Berlin, Jove was about to go to Chicago to study. He was nineteen, a dark teenage hero to a girl in old-fashioned clothes and dreaming about James Dean. We went to the trattoria to say goodbye. Mama was sad but unable to conceal her winged feet. I, no aliped, hid my lame heart.

We had a party and Raphael came with the only two of his dogs left, and Signora Rossetti wept like the Tiber and said that the good happy life had been snuffed away and the miserable dirty life had got control. There were many people who felt that way, that in spite of the war and the Crash, things had been better before the Fifties. Maybe it was Senator McCarthy's influence. During the Fifties, anyone on the outside, any kind of outside, learned to be afraid of being different. It was a decade that fell into the gap between an earlier innocence and a later tolerance. Mama said she hadn't risked her life to get out of one tyranny just to suffocate inside another. Plenty of Europeans began to think of going back home. We all knew someone who had lost their job or been put in prison for un-American activities.

Jove, Giovanni, as he was then, had twice been approached as a student by a man he had never met and offered money for information on any college students he knew who might have been Communists.

'We are not informers,' Signora Rossetti had said, when her popular Polenta Nights came under surveillance.

As one who had been followed from birth, I couldn't understand what the fuss was about.

I kissed Giovanni who gave me a dollar and a ferocious Bowie knife.

'Protect your virginity,' he said, like a mafioso, but I only heard 'ginity' and thought it was something to do with Prohibition.

'*Alla Vostra Salute!*' The party drank our health and we were gone.

Stella turned towards me and crumpled my heart in her hand.

'Do you fall in love often?'

Yes often. With a view, with a book, with a dog, a cat, with numbers, with friends, with complete strangers, with nothing at all. There are children who grow up as I did, with the love clamped down in them, who cannot afterwards love at all. There are others who make fools of themselves, loving widely, indiscreetly, forgetting it is themselves they are trying to love back to a better place.

I loved my father incestuously. I would have coupled with him in a different morality. He wanted my love but, except in small children, demonstrations of affection embarrassed him. No, it was not always so, but perhaps it is worse when love has flowed freely to find it one day dammed. When he changed I changed with him and wore a collar and lead to learn that love is not a puppy dog.

Some people dream in colour, I feel in colour, strong tones that I hue down for the comfort of the pastelly inclined. Beige and magnolia and a hint of pink are what the well-decorated heart is wearing; who wants my blood red and vein-blue?

Don't lie.

Don't lie. You know you like to view but not to buy. I have found that I am not a space where people want to live. At least not without decorating first. And that is the stubbornness in me: I do not want to be someone's neat little home. I looked round at the wrecked flat. Not answering Stella, then I said, 'I'm not in love with you.'

What would it be to love? Would it be the fields under rain, the vivid green the grass takes? Would it be the air current the bird finds? Would it be the fox and the fox hole? Would it be natural at all? Would it be lucky find or magic trick? Buried treasure or sleight of hand? Would I be the conjuror or the conjured? Would it be a spell or a song I sing?

If I am a wound would love be my salve?

If I am speechless would love be a mouth?

I do not want to declare love on you as of midnight yesterday. I do not want to be captured nor to hold a honeyed gun at your head. I do not want to spend the rest of my life as a volunteer member of the FBI. Where did you go, who did you see, what did you do today dear? I would love you as a bird loves flight, as meat loves salt, as a dog loves chase, as water finds its own level. Or I would not love you at all.

Would it be natural? You are not of my clan, not of my kind, there is no biological necessity to want you. Instincts of tribal survival do not apply. I do not want to reproduce myself nor do I need your money. You will not grant me status. You will not make my life easier. Capacity for love in its higher forms seems to be peculiarly human although even in humans it is still peculiar. This love suggests there is something beyond self-interest. The geneticists will scoff and since I cannot prove them wrong any more than they can prove themselves right, I shall only mention that scoffing is not a very scientific approach.

Am I rehearsing my arguments? Yes. My accuser is approaching.

> HE: You went to bed with my wife?

> ME: With Stella, yes.

> HE: What did you think you were playing at?

> ME: I didn't think we were playing chess.

> HE: I don't believe it.

> ME: It was sex not a miracle. (It was a miracle.)

> HE: How could you?

> ME: I didn't plan it.

Jove walked towards me, he walked away from me, he circled me as a shark does a pool of blood. Then he rang up Stella and shouted down the phone, in Italian, for two hours sixteen minutes without a pause. For the following three months he behaved like a character amalgam of Bluebeard and Coco the Clown. If he was not raging and threatening, he was cracking jokes about the man who had intended to remain a bachelor and ended up with two wives. Jove and I continued to work together, Stella and I made love together, and once a week Jove and Stella met for dinner. Emotionally balletic by nature, both were practising their lutz; in figure skating, a jump, with rotation, from the back outer edge of one skate to the back outer edge of the other. Their ice rink was my heart.

Within this arrangement of formalised Bohemianism we met all together, once a month, Jove chairing the moot, while over a Chinese takeaway we were supposed to discuss the finer points of our triune romance.

In fact, Jove tore up the bills presented to him by Stella. I returned to Jove the thirty love letters (one a day) he had written to me since our previous moot, and Jove shouted (this time at me), 'Why the hell don't you talk?'

Jove was Italian born New York raised. Stella was Jewish. Not any old Jewish but Jewish of the House of David. She was Queen Jewish, biblical Jewish, Jewish in silver and kohl. Like Jove, her forked tongue was an entire canteen of cutlery. It was not that either of them were insincere, simply that, being bored by an argument, they could change sides faster than a mercenary offered double pay. Just as I had carefully listened to each of their petitions and decided how to vote, they would somersault over each other, land on the opposite side, and finish by glaring at me. Utterly unnerved, I could not stop myself asking . . .

'Would anybody like a cup of coffee?'

I must stop saying that. World War Three is about to begin and I will be pushing the hostess trolley.

Stella looked away, flexing her fingers and rattling the bangles up her arm. She was looking away into the deserts of her ancestry, looking into the tenacity that has made her people great. She was built out of the cedars of Lebanon and inlaid with precious stones. What cared she for light refreshments?

Jove stared into space, head thrown back, English brogues under the table. He had his arms folded and he seemed to regard me as a kind of spore; a unicellular, asexual, reproductive body. Was he wrong? Every month I offered up an identical cup of coffee and had lost all trace of whatever definite sexuality I might have had. A man. His wife. The mistress of both of them. If I was tongue-tied, Jove and Stella were the ropes.

THE MOOT. ROUND ONE.

The minutes of the meeting, as taken by me, read as follows:

1) Jove insists on the rights of his penis; that is, he has fucked Stella and Alice and ought to be allowed to continue to do so.
2) Stella says that all marital rights are forfeited by an affair.
3) Jove says he is not the only one having an affair.
4) Stella disagrees:

    a) Jove is no longer having an affair. (I nod.)

    b) She, Stella, is not having an affair. She is exploring the possibilities of an alternative relationship.

    (Here there is usually a pause while they use the last of the spring rolls to mop up the prune sauce.)
5) Jove says he is not threatened by our relationship.

Stella rattles her bangles.

Jove says he would like to move back in. This is his home.

Stella pushes a variety of unpaid bills across the table.

Jove says, 'Shall I go and get my things?'

Stella says, 'No.'

Jove tears up the bills.

Stella says, 'Why don't you ask Alice how she feels?'

Jove says, 'How do you feel, Alice?'

This is the beginning of my terror. It is as though I were back at school and the hairy-nosed-tweed-bodied headmaster has said to the class, 'Alice will tell us the answer.'

After five minutes Jove says, 'Why the hell don't you talk?'

Stella says, 'Why should she talk to you, you bully?'

ROUND TWO

Jove stalks the apartment throwing things into a canvas bag. Stella circles him and picks them out again. This is symbolic only. Jove wants her to know that everything is his, she wants him to realise that it all belongs to her. Eventually . . . 'We should get a divorce.'

One or the other of them uses this gambit at 9 p.m. precisely. The food has been eaten, the contents of the apartment have been packed and unpacked.

'I'm a reasonable man,' says Jove.

'I have suffered enough,' says Stella.

What judge could find against her with her camels and her tents at her back? Jove then declares himself to be a perfect number, in other words, a number equal to the sum of its aliquot parts, in other words, he is big enough for the both of us. When he says this he can't help smirking down towards his centre. Like most men he is obsessed by the size of his member. I do not necessarily object to this vanity but I do think he should use a ruler. His priapic optimism goads Stella into some hard physiology. No he is not the biggest man she has ever met. No and not the second biggest either. Dreadfully, they turn to me, Jove's virility hanging by a thread. This is the moment, the terrible moment when I gather up the takeaway plates like a protective charm and run towards the air-raid shelter of the kitchen.

'Would anybody like a cup of coffee?'

There then followed a war-chant from Jove which should have been Olympian but was more gondolier. Visitors to Venice will recall the genial machismo shouted across the canals, the tenor/baritone of 'Who did you have last night?' There's a story that the gaily striped barber's poles that stand to moor the boats on the Grand Canal work too as notching posts. At the end of the season, the gondolier who has nosed his prow furthest wins a dinner from his comrades.

I did not mind being one of Jove's canals but I did not like being reeled off within the entire waterway. He shouted names as though he were giving directions. Perhaps that is what we were, elaborate ways for him to find himself.

When this was over, and invisible lovelies perched about the apartment in support of their god, it was Jove's habit to take one or two examples at random and give us the details of the affair. The sexual details. Heaving bosoms, flying buttocks, baby-doll sighs, massive erections. Limbs and noises were pantomimed before us with the seriousness of a travelling porno booth. Jove could have set himself up as a Punch and Judy of the groin. Perhaps it was the *commedia dell'arte* in his blood. We had to let him do this because it was the only way to exhaust him. While he performed, I washed up and Stella did the crossword.

One month, Stella looked up from One Across Two Down

and said to Jove, 'Before I met you I had a different man every night.'

'Now that I am through with you I could have a different woman every night.'

I stood in the doorless kitchen doorway and looked at them both and it was at that second that I had a queasy feeling of being nothing but a tie-beam; a beam connecting the lower ends of rafters to prevent them moving apart.

(Pause here for their monthly word-game. Jove to accuse, Stella to counter in her own defence.)

HE: Braggart.

SHE: Story-teller.

HE: Liar.

SHE: Inventor.

HE: Fantasist.

SHE: Fictioneer.

HE: Madwoman.

SHE: Poet.

HE: Deluded.

SHE: Deluder.

HE: Faker.

SHE: Illusionist.

HE: Printer's devil.

SHE: Genii.

HE: Schizophrenic.

SHE: Genius.

HE: Fork-tongued.

SHE: Mercuric.

HE: Gobbledegooker.

SHE: Runic.

HE: Legerdemain.

SHE: Linguistical.

HE: Falstaff.

SHE: Prospero.

HE: Canary.

SHE: Diva.

HE: Pot-pourrist.

SHE: Alchemist.

Jove turned to me: 'All this is your fault.'

Stella to Jove: 'Of course it isn't Alice's fault. It's your fault.'

Jove to me: 'Don't listen to her, she'll damage you. Whatever she tells you, it isn't true. What does she tell you?'

Alice to Jove: 'She tells me how you met . . .'

Jove to Alice: 'Oh that stuff, I can't talk about it . . . how we grew up together, how she left for Berlin, how she came back to the trattoria, how I was sitting there broken-hearted, looking out of the window, handsome, lonely, wondering if there was any life left, and how she . . .'

Came back to New York with a suitcase full of hope and a little money, another escapee to the tiny island, whose length and breadth has spanned the world. She knew that New York could not exist; that it was an invented city poised in the minds of its inhabitants, a hoisted dream.

She was so excited she took the elevator to the top of the Empire State Building and looked out for the city her parents had seen through the steam of the boats.

'In all the cities of this year
 I have longed for the other city.'

Her mother used to read that poem to her and think about Berlin. In Berlin the girl had read the poem and thought about New York.

'In all the rooms of this year
 I have entered one red room.'

Their apartment block had been demolished but the iron fire escape was still there, crazy, twisted, leading to nothing. She climbed it and opened the lost door to the invisible room,

Mama's red kitchen where the diamonds were. Was it here? Here that the two of them, inextricably complicit, had snuck away from the vexations of Sodom and walked through a graphite night as black as the diamond inside her was pure. Carbon: fundamental four-fold matter, coal and diamonds from the same source.

The wind rocked the unfixed ironwork and as she began to make her way down gingerly, she saw, over in the corner of the building lot, at the customary respectful distance, the dark-dressed figure waiting for her.

FOOD TASTES BETTER IN ITALIAN.

Not to Giovanni, dashing and thirty to the day. He pushed his spaghetti alla vongole round and round his plate and debated with himself what method of suicide might be the least painful and the most dramatic. Do not blame him. He was a Leo.

A divorced unemployed Leo whose anti-nuclear campaigning had finally lost him his wife, his child and his job.

In 1961 he had been angry-eyed and determined, and was one of those who had stayed out in the open in City Hall Park, when the city was ordered to practise drill for nuclear war. He was on record as a subversive because he had refused to inform for his college in the 1950s. In the 1960s, nuclear mania and Vietnam tarred him as an outsider. Only the calibre of his work had saved him from gaol and the Draft. He was necessary. His wife had thought him a coward.

Into the checked room, a good-looking woman carrying a bag. There were plenty of free tables but she sat down opposite Giovanni, smiled and pulled out a knife. He stared at her in weary amazement and with a kind of relief. If he was going to be murdered he would not have to worry about suicide.

> SHE: I did.

> HE: What?

> SHE: Protect my virginity.

They were married a couple of weeks later in St Patrick's. Divorced Catholics cannot remarry in church but for years the Fathers had eaten at the trattoria and for free. God is merciful and especially on a full stomach.

It was a happy time and no one noticed that one dark member of the congregation had not been invited.

> SHE: Do you remember, it must have been in 1958, before I went back to Berlin, and you had taken me to meet Papa at the Museum of Modern Art and a fire had broken out and burned up one of Monet's 'Waterlily' series and I was afraid and I thought I saw Papa in the fire and you snatched hold of me and promised me that no fire would come to hurt me. Do you still say that?

'Of course,' said Jove, Keeper of the Thunderbolt.

I watched them, eyes bright, afloat on history. Someone had said to me, 'Jove and Stella are inseparable.' I had smiled quietly at the time, assuming myself to be the object of desire and not the sacrifice.

What do the alchemists say? '*Tertium non datur.*' The third is not given, whatever it is that reconciles two opposites. If I was here to reconcile them were they planning to dump me overboard when the job was finished? Piratical Stella? Buccaneer Jove? Alice under the skull and crossbones of their love?

The sailing holiday planned by Jove and me was now to include Stella and me.

'No,' I thought, 'no,' but as ever with Jove, yes.

I had the expertise to hire a yacht without crew and although I would have preferred to take a cabin boy, Jove would not agree.

'No, no no. We are going away to decide our future not to be spied on by a lecherous mafioso.'

The day before we were to fly out I had a telephone call from Mother. Father had collapsed. Would I come home at once? She had booked a ticket for me on the evening plane.

I packed with one hand, made frantic calls to Jove and Stella with the other. I couldn't get hold of either of them. Finally, in a panic, wondering why the world is at its most indifferent when we are at our most desperate, I sent a fax to Jove, at the Institute, telling him what had happened and leaving my numbers in England. What could I say to Stella in the thirty-second opportunity regulated by her answer-machine?

It was two days before I tried to reach either of them again. I found they had set off as planned and had taken the yacht.

I realised that it would be possible for them to use my sailing certificates and to impersonate me. I sign myself as 'Dr' deliberately, to avoid the intrusion of Mrs? or Miss?, as if my marital status had anything to do with the rest of the world. When there is no other evidence it is assumed I am a man. Inevitably.

It would not be the first time that Jove and Stella had covered the traces of where I began and where they ended. I liked the playfulness of the lovers' argument: who are you and who am I? Which of us is which? Liked it less when the erotic twinhood devolved into forged letters and faked signatures.

It had begun as a game. Post-coital ludos lathered with champagne. Bubbling with love I had shown Jove how to calligraph himself as me. If he could turn his wrist to mine, he might become me, he might free me. If he could be let go into myself, then I might be let loose into another self. He might displace me as a heavy solid displaces water.

At the time, I did not find this analogy sinister.

Once upon a time there were two friends who found a third. Liking no one better in the whole world, they vowed to live in one palace, sail in one ship, and fight one fight with three arms.

After three months they decided to go on a quest.

'What shall we seek?' they asked each other.

The first said, 'Gold.'

The second said, 'Wives.'

The third said, 'That which cannot be found.'

They all agreed that this last was the best and so they set out in fine array.

After a while they came to a house that celebrated ceilings and denied floors. As they marched through the front door they were only just in time to save themselves from dropping into a deep pit. While they clung in terror to the wainscoting, they looked up and saw chandeliers, bright as swords, that hung and glittered and lit the huge room where the guests came to and fro. The room was arranged for dinner, tables and chairs suspended from great chains, an armoury of knives and forks laid out in case the eaters knocked one into the abyss.

There was a trumpet sound and the guests began to enter the room through a trap door in the ceiling. Some were supported on wires, others walked across ropes slender as youth. In this way they were able to join their place setting. When all were assembled, the trumpet blew again, and the head of the table looked down and said to the three friends, 'What is it you seek?'

'That which cannot be found.'

'It is not here,' she answered, 'but take this gold,' and each of the diners threw down a solid gold plate, rather in the manner that the Doge of Venice used to throw his dinnerware into the canal to show how much he despised worldly things.

Our three friends did not despise worldly things and caught as many of the plates as they could. Loaded down with treasure they continued on their way, although more slowly than before.

Eventually they came to Turkey and to the harem of Mustapha the Blessed CIXX. Blessed he was, so piled with ladies that only his index finger could be seen. Crooking it, he bade the friends come forward, and asked in a muffled voice, 'What is it you seek?'

'That which cannot be found.'

'It is not here,' he said in a ghostly smother, 'but take some wives.'

The friends were delighted, but observing the fate of Mustapha, they did not take too many. Each took six and made them carry the gold plate.

Helter-skelter down the years the friends continued their journey, crossing continents of history and geography, gathering by chance the sum of the world, so that nothing was missing that could be had.

At last they came to a tower in the middle of the sea. A man with the face of centuries and the voice of the wind opened a narrow window and called . . .

'What is it you seek?'

'That which cannot be found . . . found . . . found,' and the wind twisted their voices into the air.

'It has found you,' said the man.

They heard a noise behind them like a scythe cutting the water and when they looked round they saw a ship thin as a blade gaining towards them. The figure rowed it standing up, with one oar, but it was not an oar. They saw the curve of the metal flashing, first this side, and then that. They saw the rower throw back his hood. They saw him beckon to them and the world tilted. The sea poured away.

Who are they with fish and starfish in their hair?

DEATH

June 8 1960. Liverpool, England. Sun in Gemini.

My father at the wheel of the *Godspeed*. Myself birthed and bloody in my mother's fur. The creosoted cabin, the paraffin lamp. Smell of oil, tar, sardines and gin.

I flew into London Heathrow and when the Customs officer asked me if I had anything to declare, I said, 'My father is dying.'

I took a connecting flight to Liverpool and a taxi to my grandmother's house, the old two up two down nearby the defeated docks.

Grandmother always had seemed fabulously old, unicorn old, strange figure out of time. Now she was biblically old, upright as a prophet, sharp-tongued as the Serpent himself. She opened the front door as if it were the Hall of Judgement. Perhaps it was.

'David's asleep,' she said. 'Your mother's drunk.'

★

I went inside and through to the kitchen. It had been carpeted, tiled, formica'd, glassed, and beside the coal range was a built-in gas cooker. I looked around for the rabbit. Gone.

'The Social Services,' said Grandmother, pronouncing it KGB. 'They said, "Do it up or go into a home. Not fit for human habitation." I said I am human and I have inhabited it for more than sixty years.'

We sat down at what kitchen shops call the breakfast bar.

'I should be dead,' said Grandmother. 'I should be dead not David.'

I listened to her story of what had happened, running it back through my mind to where it had begun. I had seen my father put off his bright self and shroud himself in dead men's clothes, the pressure suit and pressure helmet of normal life. When at last he was fully dressed in the ways of the world he had pumped up the suit with an inflation of respectability. He had protected himself against himself. His pressure suit saved him from the disruptive forces of depth.

At the same time he began to corrode inside it. His first crisis, when I was nine, and we had moved to London to jump ship at the death of the docks, re-detonated the action man inside him. He became a cartoon of his vigorous positive self. At the moment of decline accelerate. He dragged himself out of shadow into a twenty-four-hour day. He had successfully made the transition from the old-fashioned values of the post-war world into the edginess of modern life. He was admirable, my father, admirable and brave, and unable to see that the shadow he so feared was his own.

During the seeming sunshine years his shadow lengthened. Fixedly gazing ahead, my father pretended not to notice. He did not notice that the sun on the sun-dial told a different story to the one he was telling himself. He had to be a hero under a high noon. The light should not waver or wane. He forgot that time processes. Fatally he did not remember that by some loop in its own laws, time can precess. My father got older and younger at the same time. As he became more senator-like, the wild boy, the dock boy, my tug-boat father, rioted, though well below the protection of consciousness.

He started to complain of a twitch. The doctor gave him tablets. At board meetings, at his most imperious, leading the good men in grey, he twitched. One side of him remained dignified and upright. The other side leapt galvanically. He was advised to take time off. He refused.

At the Cunard birthday celebrations my father twitched a full bottle of Krug over HRH Duke of Edinburgh.

'A Greek,' said my grandmother, pronouncing it 'Who?'

The board retired him. It was no disgrace. He was comfortably in his sixties and could have chosen to leave on his own account. His chauffeur collected him on his last afternoon as himself, and asked, as usual, 'Where to, Sir?'

'Liverpool,' said my father.

As the Jaguar spun the motorway under its wheels my father wondered why the road should not go on forever. What was his destination? Who was driving? There was the familiar outline at the wheel. Himself in the back assuming he had control. He had made himself passenger of his own life.

He leaned forward to tap on the window. He wanted to tell the driver that he would prefer to get out and walk. He fell back, shaking himself. Get out and walk? He was going to Liverpool. What was the matter with him?

'Be someone. Be someone.' His mother's words tattooed on his body, his secret skin worn under an expensive suit.

'I am someone,' he said out loud. 'But who?'

How he had hated the two up two down terraced house. How he had hated his own father, coarse, suspicious. How much guilty relief he had felt when his father had been torpedoed.

A year before his father was killed, he had come home after a gas accident in his submarine. What should have been a container of oxygen had corrupted his lungs into a rebellion of mucus and blood. He had recovered but his left side was permanently damaged. The nerves and skin clung to him in a pantomime of life that was not life. His lidded eye, his drooping mouth, the wasted, twitching arm and his leg in his boot fastened so tight that it seemed to be there to hold the leg on.

David remembered having to sit on his knee and dive for sweets in his dead pocket.

His father was given a clean bill of health by the Navy doctor who wanted him back in the submarine. The night before he left, he crept up to David, asleep in bed, and bent down, a bandana tied over his face, whispering 'It's in the air, lad, it's in the air. Can you not smell it? It's in the air.'

David could smell it. The thick soaked uniform smeared with blood and urine. The stale water. The smell of death and destruction. The smell of a stretcher and a dirty red blanket. If the horror is inside you how do you get it out?

In the terraced house David learned not to breathe.

★

When his father was killed David felt a rush of air in his lungs. He breathed so hard that he feared his nostrils would jam with wardrobes and chairs. His bellow lungs opened so wide his nose could not supply them. Would he die with every piece of house furniture packed into his respiratory tract? He leaned out of the window trying to breathe in the whole sky. In the morning his mother's bedding plants had been uprooted from the garden by a violent wind.

He loved his mother. He would be someone.

David got out of the effortless Jaguar and handed his chauffeur £1,000 in cash. He shook him by the hand, thanked him, and turned away, upright, untwitching, towards the buildings that had been Trident Shipping. His chauffeur reversed quickly and drove away. The car had to be cleaned and ready that evening for David's successor.

David went into the old buildings that his mother had cleaned from 1928 until 1978 and where he had started work in 1947. The sheds, stores, wharf-ends and offices had been converted into an art gallery, theatre space and healthy-eating café. David walked across the shiny floors and puzzled over the installation of wire netting and lifelike plastic cod. Out of place among the jeans and baseball caps, the man in the Savile Row overcoat ordered a piece of carrot cake and a cup of strong tea. A group of students glanced over at him.

'Who do they think I am?' he wondered. 'A rich stupid old man.' And he laughed because he had been poorer than any of them and cleverer too.

'This used to be the clerks' office,' he said out loud. (The students looked up and then looked away.) 'There were twelve of us in here. We used to call it the Apostles' Shift. Every week the company stopped a shilling off our wages to pay for the suits we wore.' (He paused.) 'A shilling. Might as well say a doubloon. All in the past. History, I suppose.'

He thought about it. Getting old was not something he had expected. He wanted to say, 'Why am I old?' and although he knew that question had no meaning, it had meaning to him. His body and his mind, allies for so long, had begun to quarrel. And his spirit? Where was his spirit in this new parting of the ways? He didn't believe in God but occasionally, uncomfortably, he had a sense that God believed in him.

'I am a stupid old man,' he thought.

He took out his book. *Other People: A Mystery Story*.

He had been attracted by the title because it seemed to him that other people were mysterious, unknown. He got along by making assumptions about them, they got along by making assumptions about him. How much of any of that was true? The students had glanced at him and looked away. They thought they knew what he was, in so much as he was anything at all to them. He had his own impressions of them; lazy, shallow, scruffy, dull. *He* hadn't been to university and look at him now.

'Yes,' he thought. 'Look at me now. Why not? It tells us nothing we need to know.' He wished he could go and speak to them. He wished he could say, 'I am not that man you see sitting in the corner. My name is David.'

He looked at his feet under the table. He did not see his polished Oxfords and dark wool socks, he saw thick-soled boots with steel tips, heels hooked over the spindle of a clerk's high stool. A fluffy cotton mop pushed his feet back into the present.

'Mind yer feet, please.'

'Mother?'

'David.'

He furrowed his face at her. She had not worked here for twenty years. What was happening to him?

It was his mother, stuffed into her pink overall like a prune inside a wrap of bacon.

'I'm doing the cleaning.'

She sat opposite him, KGB in her voice.

'Pretend you don't know me.'

The students nudged one another and a girl giggled.

'What are you doing here?' she said. 'You'll get me into trouble.'

'I retired today,' he said, and the words sounded far off. Someone else's.

'Well I'm still working and if they find out you're my son I'll lose my job.'

'Why?' He didn't understand.

'Look at the age of you. I told them I was sixty-one.'

Sixty-one. Sixty-one. She was nearly ninety. Anyone could see that she was nearly ninety. Her stomach had slipped to her thighs. Her breasts had slipped to her stomach. Her neck was in her vest. Her chin was in her neck and her eyes had receded so far into her hollow skull that from the camouflage of her thin hair she should have been able to see backwards.

'You look nothing like sixty-one.'

She simpered and blushed. 'You always were a good son.'

'Let me take you home.'

'If you want to wait you can. I finish at six o'clock.'

Six o'clock. He stood in the dismal staff room while his mother hung up her pink overall in the grey metal locker. She put on her hat and coat and slipped her arm through his. Together they walked out towards the water. She took the wharf way home. A street lamp shone into the opaque river leaving an orange reflection. He thought of her polishing the brass plaques and how he fancied he had seen the fire of them, once, a long time ago in the harbour of New York. His secretary, Uta, had told him a story about her own soul flashing across the waters towards her. He had been surprised. That was not the sort of woman she seemed to be; so practical, so self-contained. Beautiful to a young man away from home. He had given her presents, clothes, perfume. And there was a night when . . .

He pushed the memories aside. After he had left New York she had sent him a tie. Silk. Red with white spots. It had worn through with wearing it, he had worn it for so many years. He kept it though, in the drawer with his handkerchiefs. A piece of time worn through.

Arm in arm, David and his mother, walking together as they used to walk when he waited for her to finish work and cook him kippers juggled down from their rack in the chimney. He could taste them, and his happiness, both warm in his mouth.

'Where are you staying?' she said.

'With you?'

They walked. Walked slowly past the rusted rings where the ships tethered. Walked by the packing depots empty as cathedrals. They walked by the pub with the pianola. Walked by the new gift shops selling candlesticks made out of salvaged railings. 'People are not recyclable,' he thought. 'I should enjoy being melted down into something new.' For the splinter of a second, his mind, luminous, reached forward. Then he checked himself as he always did. Nothing. Nothing. Nothing. The night was dark.

They went in. He felt a sense of relief and irresponsibility. This was his boyhood home. This was his mother's house. His sea-boots were still in the cupboard, the exhausted rubber thin as skin. His pea-coat was behind the door. Nobody would come for him here.

He found his blue roll-neck sweater, incongruous over the trousers of his suit, but he pulled it on anyway. His mother watched him as she mashed the potatoes.

He ate with his elbows on the table. Eating with his fork in his right hand. She poured him a glass of Guinness.

While she ate her own meal she silently answered her own question. 'You would not have been any happier, David, if you had stayed here with the other men.'

She told me that, later, almost in self-defence. I took her hand. If my father had not been haunted by an imagined past, he would have been haunted by an imagined future. Standing still, he would have envied movement. Moving, he longed to stand still. He was not a dissatisfied man. He was a man who could never quite learn the lines he had scripted for himself. Even at his most enthusiastic for a role, some part of him could not forget that it was a role. He did not know how to merge himself into one. A little less consciousness, or a little more, might have saved him. As it was he suffered.

He was ashamed of suffering. Well-off people were not allowed to feel suffering. When they did, it became a kind of public hanging, exposed to the 'Serve him right' fascination of the crowd. He wondered, idly, if there should be some Government guidelines on how much a person could have in the bank and still be allowed to suffer.

He was a self-made man. He was a blue-collar boy who could afford a tailor. He thought of himself as working class but other people found that absurd. The company he kept was well-off stock from well-off stock. They were the ones in positions of power. They were the ones who succeeded to control just as the aristocracy succeeded to title. The right homes, the right schools, the right connections, the right expectations. All of that was rewarded and when a man like him broke in through the window and took his place at the table, he had to be twice as good and still they made light of his achievements. Still would not quite believe that he was a street boy with a scholarship and more yearning than they knew was in the whole world. They acted as though it was just a fluke that more people like him weren't in the same position as so many people like them. And sometimes they hinted he had had it easy. And sometimes, quite openly, they called him a thug. He had energy, no one could deny that, and a mission about him, that frankly, they found vulgar. They wanted to like him but he just wasn't a likeable man. Too awkward, too angled, too arrogant, too proud. Odd that he got on so well with the workforce.

He was lonely. None of his friends, his own kind, his own type, had done as well as he had. He had sailed away from that life and there was no passage of return. When he met people he had known, the downtrodden ones were overawed and the middle-class failures patronised him. He had been lucky of course. Of course. And now he was an island unto himself visited for goods and water.

His wife was an alcoholic. His fault he knew. His children had been brought up with the right schools, the right connections, the right expectations. They hardly ever visited. And Alice, whom he loved, had turned out to be three times as good, and hated him, he thought, for what he had become.

It was over now, suffering and striving. He had re-made his Will, leaving his wife their house and more than enough money. The rest, his shares, investments, capital, he had put into trust as scholarship money for poor children. One of them, maybe, would manage what he had not, and make sense of the contradictions.

He washed his plate, kissed his mother, and went upstairs to the little room where he had slept. It was cold but he did not care. He lay in bed, listening to his mother stacking the pots and pans. His right side felt heavy and numb. His left side, lighter, freer. He usually held it rigid in fear of the twitch. It was a dog he had to muzzle.

He slept and in his dreams he was steering the *Godspeed* again and his wife had given birth to his daughter and he had lit the river red with flares. Further back, and he was in New York taking his secretary on the ferry to Staten Island. He had held her hand, and later they had made love in a children's animal park. Further back, and he was courting his own wife, black hair blue eyes and Irish green in the wit of her. Was that him, dashing, untidy, and full of promise? He had promised . . . he had lied.

Trident Shipping. A young man with ruddy cheeks, never quite at ease on an office stool. A young man spending his summer evenings loading the ships with his mates. Sam! Ted! He called them but they did not hear. David! His other self did not turn round. He tried to follow David home, but the man was not himself, it was a lad, eleven or twelve, in a smart uniform on his way to a fee-paying school. David waited for the lad all day long, and saw him at last, returning, dejected, confused, with a cut over his eye. The boy kissed his mother, threw his satchel into a corner and ran out to play. 'Your uniform, David. Your uniform.' Her voice was lost. The lad was in bed now, breathing steady, in, out, breathing through time.

In the night David had a stroke. In the morning he was paralysed on his right side. He could not call out. He could not speak.

I sat by my father's bed, holding his hand, thinking him, feeling him, not knowing how else to communicate. He was not dead but he had no life. This was the room I had slept in on those years of party nights. I did not expect to see my father in the same narrow bed.

'He won't know you,' said Grandmother. Would he not? His brain and his body were speaking different languages now and there was no interpreter between. If I talked to him would he understand?

I began to tell him a story. A story of mirrors and handkerchiefs, of winter and New York. Of a man I had wanted to marry, of his wife whom I loved. Of spaghetti and numbers, paintings and the Algonquin Hotel. The Ship of Fools, and he and I on it.

I should have preferred it to be neater, tauter, the pace of a mystery, the thrill of a romance. What I had were fragments of coloured glass held up to the light . . . This is my signal flashing towards you.

It was a strange Confessional chamber. My father was as invisible and remote as a priest. What I could not have told him in life, I told him in this absence of life. I poured my brimming heart into the huge space of him. Tears pressed under his closed eyelids and filled the gutters of his cheeks. His tears, his fluid self. My father washed back into the river that had made him. The waters claiming him at last. *Rheingeld*. The gold in him unhardened as sun on

154

the water. I thought we were hand in hand again, picking over the jetsam of the tide, able to speak, my father and I. To say what it was and to forgive.

He died in the oval of his tears.

My mother insisted that the funeral tea be served at the Hotel Ra-Ra (décor Merseyside-Egypt). The hotel, that had catered for the shipping trade in its handsomer days now wrung a living out of salesman incentive weekends and marketing days for the frozen-fish industry. It had a sorrow about it unrelieved by the magnificent marble steps and Lalique lamps. Its kitsch Anubis lay exhausted in the foyer and its replica of Cleopatra's Needle had been patched with aluminium foil. Our tea had been laid out in the Pharaoh Room. Drinks were in the Pyramid Bar.

'Once there was nowhere like it,' said my mother.

Once? She had stayed in enough hotels to realise that there could never be anywhere like it. Benefiting from its frozen-fish connections, the hotel was offering mummified prawns, ice still clinging to their carcasses as though they were waiting to be rejuvenated in the next century. After the prawns came the sandwiches. Funeral Sandwiches on specially ordered black rye bread. I read the list. Egg. Egg and tomato. Egg and cress. Egg Mersey. When I asked the waitress about Egg Mersey she told me with Nefertiti hauteur that it was egg without the yolk.

'Hard-boiled-egg-white sandwiches?'

'Suit yourself.'

As I progressed up the meal table I found the disappeared yolks. Each yolk had been cut in halves and stood, dome up, on a platter. This was called Egg Peaks.

'What a lot of egg,' I said to no one in particular.

'There was a mix-up,' said Nefertiti. 'I was told you were Merry Hen.'

'Merry Hen?'

'"Britain's Brightest Egg". It's their conference tomorrow.'

'And today is my father's funeral.'

I left her, nonplussed, defensive, and went over to my grandmother who was sitting alone beneath a browned palm tree. She had a plate of Funeral Sandwiches and a glass of sherry.

'I'm sorry,' I said.

'It doesn't matter.'

No. It doesn't matter. The funeral is for the living not the dead. It would have amused my father to see the grey and guilty men flocking round my mother in the Pyramid Bar.

'There's worse to come,' she said.

She meant the Will. She had told me what my father had done. My sisters, who had married richly, expected to be richer still. As Jane Austen heroines everywhere, they were perfumed with love but smelled money. Tomorrow we would have to go to London for the reading of the Will.

'Let's go home.'

We reversed through the fire-door behind Grandmother's chair. Outside, the streets were busy with shoppers, and it was neither the blaring plate-glass nor the deadly absurdities of the Hotel Ra-Ra that made me feel giddy but the space in between them. The engulfing space between flat earth and tilted earth. The space where I could fall and float between their lives and mine.

Death the Revealer. When he throws back his hood what is it that he uncovers? His face or ours? Our faces usually hid from one another behind assumption and complacency. Our faces turned away even when our bodies are turned near. Do I want to look at you, afraid of what I might see? I prefer to look through you, round you, with you, anything to avoid the intensity of one single face. And will you look at me, hood thrown back, vulnerable? They did, curiously, unnerved, and looked away quickly. There was something wrong with that woman. They saw me raw. They drew their own hoods tighter. Death the Revealer in my liquid stare.

Walk with me. Hand in hand through the nightmare of narrative. Need to tell a story when no story can be told. Walk the level reassuring floor towards the open trapdoor. Plank by plank to where the sea begins. This is a sea story, a wave story, a story that breaks and ebbs, spilling the boat up on the beach, dragging it out to a tiny dot. Life asail on its own tears.

Walk the plank. The rough, springy underfoot of my emotions. The 'I' that I am, subjective, hesitant, goaded from behind, afraid of what lies ahead, the drop, the space, the gap between other people and myself.

Hear me. Speak to me. Look at me.

'Look at me,' said Grandmother. Yes look at her. Spiny as a jujube tree, sweet as a julep, ju-jitsu-minded with a heart like a jubilee. Energy, work and heat in the joule-force of her. A wryneck jynx, sudden turn of the head. Woodpecker bird at the World Ash Tree.

We were walking home. Everybody else playing Saturday donkey, pannier laden either side with vegetables and meat. The queues at the bus-stop, the shop-neon switching off, the roar of the garbage trucks clearing forests of cardboard. All this familiar and far away.

I wanted to buy something the way I want to flex my fingers when they are chilled. Still there? All still there? Normal, and I a part of it. If all these lives are as before why not mine?

I stopped and got a couple of Mars Bars from a paper-stand.

'Old lady hungry is she?' said the vendor. I thought he meant the chocolate and I glanced at Grandmother walking like a question mark beside me. I was holding her hand and in the other she was holding the plate of Funeral Sandwiches from the Hotel Ra-Ra. Gently, I put them on the pavement and we walked on.

My father used to do magic tricks. His favourite was to flounce a red silk handkerchief over a tumbler of water and toss it at one of his friends. As they stepped back in dismay, expecting to be doused, the handkerchief fluttered harmlessly at their feet, no trace of the airborne H_2O.

How was it done? My father never performed this trick unless he was standing behind a desk or table where he had prudently pinned a servante. A servante, out of sight, and in line with the magician's testicles, is a deep pocket designed to contain the debris of the last trick and the essentials of the one to follow. While my father made great play of arranging his handkerchief over the glass, he dropped the glass into the servante. The shape of the already vanished tumbler was maintained by a metal ring, like a large cock ring, sewn into the double thickness of the handkerchief. To the observer, the ring is the rim of the glass, and so, when the handkerchief is pirouetted into the air, the glass seems to have disappeared.

He terrorised my mother by insisting on whipping the table-cloth off the table when it had been set for dinner. As children we adored such Mephistophelean disregard for order, the scandalised cups and plates flung against gravity into a Madhatter's party. Sometimes my father said it was the table that had been spirited away, and that the saucers, knives, forks and jugs re-settled in their proper place, had only the tablecloth on which to depend.

Perhaps he was right. Perhaps there is no table. Perhaps the firm surface of order and stability is as much an illusion as a silk handkerchief over a non-existent glass. Glass and table have long since disappeared but the shape remains convincing. At least until we learn how it is done.

If the Superstring theory is correct there is no table. There is no basic building block, no firm stable first principle on which to pile the rest. The cups and saucers are in the air, the cloth levitating under them, the table itself is notional, we would feel uncomfortable eating our dinner without it, in fact it is a vibration as unsolid as ourselves.

Where is my father? Meaningless question, he would say, but it has meaning for me, who has buried what I thought of as him, his solid self. The firm surface of my father on which we piled the rest. The statue of Atlas holding up the world, but what holds up Atlas, as the old conundrum goes?

My father was his own conjuring trick; the impression of something solid when what was solid had vanished away. He had become his clothes. He had become his job. It was as though he had tunnelled into another life without telling anyone, including himself. I imagine him, vigorous, unconcerned, in a wilder place, cheating us here with a lacquered offering of respectability, his painted funeral mask wheeled through the streets while he had reassembled himself on the other side of the wall. Stuff of science fiction? If there are parallel universes my authentic father could have been living on any one of them, leaving us with his distorted self.

Infinite grace. Infinite possibility. The mercy of the universe extended in its own laws. According to quantum theory there are not only second chances, but multiple chances. Space is not simply connected. History is not unalterable. The universe itself is forked. If we knew how to manipulate space-time as space-time manipulates itself the illusion of our single linear lives would collapse. And if our lives here are not the total our death here will not be final.

I play with these things to free myself from common sense, which tells me, not least, that I experience the earth as flat and my father as dead. He may be less dead now than he has been for thirty years. My grandmother's old-fashioned religious comfort of an afterlife may not be as soft-headed as some believe. As an arm-chair atheist I stumble into God as soon as I get up and walk. I do not know what God is, but I use it as a notation of value.

God = highest value. Force and freedom of the thinking universe. The model of the universe as mechanical has no basis in fact. In a quantum universe, heaven and hell are simply parallel possibilities. In our Judeo-Christian myth-world, Eve ate the apple. In a symmetrical myth-world next door, Eve did not. Paradise lost. Paradise unlost. Objections to this are logical but quantum mechanics is not interested in our logic. Every quantum experiment conducted has shown, again and again, with dismaying mischief, that particles can hold positions contradictory and simultaneous.

'If we ask whether the position of the electron remains the

same we must say no. If we ask whether the electron's position changes with time, we must say no. If we ask whether the electron is at rest we must say no. If we ask whether it is in motion we must say no.'   (Robert Oppenheimer)

Where is my father? The decay of him is buried. Impossible that he should be alive and dead at the same time. Quantum theory states that for every object there is a wave function that measures the probability of finding that object at a certain point in space and time. Until the measurement is made, the object (particle) exists as a sum of all possible states. The difficulty here, between the logical common sense world and the complex, maverick universe, is that at a sub-atomic level, matter does not exist, with certainty, in definite places, rather it has a *tendency to exist*. At the sub-atomic level, our seeming-solid material world dissolves into wave-like patterns of probabilities, and these patterns do not represent probabilities of things but probabilities of connection. Atlas 0 Ariadne 1. The hard-hat bull-nose building blocks of matter, manipulated by classical physics, now have to be returned as an infinite web of relationships. What is chosen and why is still unknown.

A wave function spreads indefinitely, though at its farthest it is infinitesimally flimsy. Theoretically, it was always possible, though unlikely, to find my father beyond the solar system, his clustered energies elsewhere. More obviously, my father seemed to be here, as you and I are here, but we too can be measured as wave functions, unlimited by the boundaries of our bodies. What physicists identify as our wave function may be what has traditionally been called the soul. My father, at the moment of physical death, may simply have shifted to an alternative point of his wave function. What my grandmother believes in and I speculate upon, seems only to be a difference in terminology. She hopes he is in heaven. I hope he has found the energy to continue along his own possibility.

Sceptical? The laws of physics concern themselves with what is possible not what is practical.

The property of matter and light is very strange. How can we accept that everything can be, at the same time, an entity confined in volume (a particle) and a wave spread out over huge regions of space? This is one of the paradoxes of quantum theory, or as the Hindu mystics put it centuries ago, 'smaller than small, bigger than big'. We are and we are not our bodies.

If we accept Hawking's idea that we should treat the entire universe as a wave function, both specifically located and infinite, then that function is the sum of all possible universes, dead, alive, multiple, simultaneous, interdependent, co-existing. Moreover, 'we' and the sum universe cannot be separated in the way of the old Cartesian dialectic of 'I' and 'World'. Observer and observed are part of the same process. What did Paracelsus say? 'The galaxa goes through the belly.'

What is it that you contain? The dead, time, light patterns of millennia, the expanding universe opening in your gut. No longer confined by volume, my father is free to choose the extent of himself. Is that him, among the stars and starfish of different skies?

This is how I explain it. My mother drinks. My grandmother reads the Bible, my sisters numb themselves in excess family life. To each his own epidural. It does ease the pain but the pain persists, the dull ache, low down as though my back had been broken and not properly healed. Perhaps it would be better to lie on his grave like a dog. To howl out the plain fact that there is no comfort, no relief, that grief must be endured until it has exhausted itself on me. My mind repeats its exercises like a lesson-book. Over and over the same ground, memories, happiness, the said and unsaid, the last hours, helplessness of the living, autonomy of the dead.

'He is not dead,' I say to myself, renouncing the word because it is imprecise.

'David is dead,' says my grandmother, over and over, with the finality of a bell.

We looked at each other, afraid to speak, afraid to load our feelings into words in case the words cracked and split. I pinned my tongue to the roof of my mouth. Hold in, hold in, one crack and the wall is breached. I need now to be finite, self-contained, to stop this bacterial grief dividing and multiplying till its weight is the weight of the world. Bacteria: agents of putrefaction. My father's decay lodged in me. Fed on, what is vital is sapped. I decrease. It increases. Bowel to brain of me, this pain. What words? What words can I trust to convey this fragile heart?

Stopper it up, heart and words, give the pain nothing to feed on. Still now, my still heart. I will counterfeit death as my father counterfeited life. On that continuum we meet.

Grandmother and I sat face to face over the sepulchral plastic of the breakfast bar. Common and rare, to sit face to face like this. Common that people do, rare that they understand each other. Each speaks a private language and assumes it to be the lingua franca. Sometimes words dock and there is a cheer at port and cargo to unload and such relief that the voyage was worth it. 'You understand me then?'

I wanted her to understand me. I wanted to find a word, even one, that would have the same meaning for each of us. A word not bound and sealed in dictionaries of our own. 'Though I speak with tongues of men and angels but have not love . . .'

'I love you.'

She nodded. 'Can we get rid of all this, do you think?'

She meant the kitchen. The breakfast bar was easy to demolish and I unscrewed all those handy flat-packed chipboard and formica cupboards and put them in a pile in the yard. I went out and bought some coal and we lit the range again, filthy, black, smoky, unhygienic, red eye laughing at us. We carried in the scrubbed-elm table and the big dresser. Underneath the acrylic floor covering were the polished stone tiles.

'They'll put you in a home,' I said.

'This is my home and it was David's and it will be yours when I die.'

When I die. The words running forward into the future. For now, her home, her way of life. Too much had been taken away already.

'This is how I want it,' she said. 'So that I can remember.' She heaved herself under the sink and brought out the formaldehyde rabbit. 'It was David who bottled this.' We put it back on the dresser shelf, its ears bobbing against its lid.

Love bears all things, believes all things, hopes all things, endures all things. Love never ends.

THE MOON

A yacht sailing off Capri was last sighted on Sunday June 16 at
18:00 hours. The boat was in difficulties. Severe storms prevented rescue attempts for 24 hours. It is thought that the boat
could be drifting at sea.

Am I dead? Dead as in doornail. Dead as in to the world. Dead as
in gone. Dead as in buried. Dead as a dodo, dead as a herring, dead
as mutton, dead as in left for?

We heard the bulletin when our short-wave radio spat into life.
Through the crackle and the static came news of our death. Jove,
with his head-cans and his screwdriver has been trying to tap back
a message but the frequency is jammed. We can listen in but we
can't call out. I heard some Mozart this morning, '*Madamina, il*

catalogo e questo/Delle belle che amo il padron mio.' (Dear lady, this is a list of the beauties my master has loved.)

Dead as in dead in his arms? Before we left I had a note from Alice saying she would be joining us at the port in a few days. When she did not arrive, Jove levered me into signing for the boat. 'Nothing to it,' he said. 'Just a rudder and an engine.'

At first it was plain sailing. Bobbing boat. Blue lagoon. Fishing, coffee, safe outline of the coast and other vessels hailing us. When the sea took the colour of clotted blood from the setting sun bleeding into it, we noticed the shallower swimming fish fast-finning it below the waves. We did not understand that they were using the deep water as a shelter. The sea had become lake-like, flat enough to walk on, a miracle sea and we two pilgrims in our little boat.

'A voyage of self-discovery,' said Jove. What I discovered, as the boat reared up like a rocket and gravity abandoned us, was that Jove had written the note from Alice. He clung to the cabin stove, screwed in to the deck and begged me to forgive him. He had remembered he was a Catholic and he was afraid to face death with a deception round his neck.

'You bastard,' I shouted, my body covered with crockery. 'You stupid selfish bastard.' And I found out that Alice had gone because her father was dying. My heart tore.

Is this how it ends? When Papa died, Mama was having an affair with a man she worked for and I was supposed not to know. Papa was supposed not to know. Mama did not believe in life after death, she wanted her life before death. She hated the enclosed space she trod like a tethered animal. Her anger. Papa's sorrow. His death when his heart wore too thin for his body.

'Look for me,' he said. 'As you are used to do and do not be deceived by a shape you no longer recognise.'

'I want to be free,' said Mama, but Papa's was the escape.

'How did he die?' Alice had asked me, when we were stacking up our life histories as a bulwark against the world. That which is shared by us. That which is not shared by you.

'He bled himself to death.'

When Papa had visited the cardiologist he had learned that his condition was rare. In most cases the failing heart thickens. The blood itself, sullen and unriverlike flows insufficiently, delaying the pumping, changing, purifying process that the body needs for its self-regulation. The heart's remedy is to work harder. Eventually the strain will prove too great. In Papa's case, the normal cardiac cycle of seventy-four completions per minute had doubled. His blood, thin and wild, hurtled through his body at waterfall rate. The valves of the heart and of the great vessels open and close according to the pressure within the chambers of the heart. Papa should have exploded. His heart was working too hard, but for reasons entirely contrary to the usual. Papa's system was running at inhuman capacity. His blood pressure, the force exerted by the blood on the walls of the blood vessels that contain it, was such that we could see the blood, tidal in the arteries and veins, sweeping Papa in and out.

The pulse is described as a wave of distension and elongation felt in an artery wall due to the contraction of the left ventricle forcing about 90 millilitres of blood into the already full aorta. When I put my fingers on Papa's wrist to take his pulse, it felt as though someone were hammering at my hand. So violent was the pulse rate that I had to use my thumb as a gripper to prevent my fingers being thrown back at my face.

'Nibelung,' said Mama, thinking of Wagner's dwarfs that hammer under the surface of the earth in The Ring.

I went with Papa up to his room of the shawls and boxes and precious stones and he told me that he had been experimenting to increase his body's revolutions. He wanted to transcend the illusion of matter. In the 1920s and 1930s, before he had fled Austria, Papa had corresponded with many of the scientists who were trying to understand, through quantum theory, what the world might really be like. He had been close to Werner Heisenberg whose strange notions of the simultaneous absence and presence of matter had stimulated Papa into investigations of his own. In the paradoxes of Kabbalah he found the paradoxes of new physics. When Heisenberg told him that every object can be understood as a point (finite, bounded, specific) and as a wave function (spreading infinitely though concentrated at different rates), Papa wanted to discover whether or not he could move himself along his own wave function, at will, whilst alive in his body. If gross matter is reducible to atoms, and the atom itself subject to unending division, then the reality of matter is conceptual. The method of Kabbalah is to free the individual from conceptual frameworks, which are all and always provisional. Could Papa escape himself by himself? Could he be his own gateway?

And so began the years of mutterings and singing, of prayer and meditation, of jewels and dusty books, of Mama's saucepans and conversations through the night. Where better than New York, city of invention and re-invention, the autobiography of the immigrant that re-writes itself as a fiction? The fictions that pass the thin walls of reality and assume a different kind of truth. New York, the perfect paradox. Stable and unstable, degraded and glorious. A Scheherazade of a city, full of tales told and to be told, a city of concrete and glass that lives by its dreams.

★

The doctor had told Papa that he would soon be dead. By convention he was dead. The economy of his body had become extravagant. Too overblown to sustain life, he was, by every prediction and indicator, dead. The only objection to this analysis was Papa himself.

As we talked, of the snow-filled winter, of my birth, of his studies, of Mama, I realised he was saying goodbye to me. I was a child, I did not know how to stop him, how to speak to him. I was as helpless as when Mama took me as a decoy to her lover's rendezvous. The adult world still happened to me. I was not a part of it.

Then he sent me home, away from the bookstore and back to our apartment. Mama was angry because I was late for supper and because she wanted to go out.

Through the night I was troubled by pictures, fragments of pictures, and I seemed to be with Papa, walking on his nights of search. We were alone and the city was red.

In the morning, when Mama went to the bookstore, she found Papa, neatly bled to death in a galvanised bathtub he kept in his room. He was pale as a plaster icon, his pounded body white with stillness. He had been reading, as his life as we knew it drained away. Mama picked up the book. It was a new collection from a poet he admired: Muriel Rukeyser, *Body of Waking* (1958). She looked at the page.

KING'S MOUNTAIN

In all the cities of this year
I have longed for the other city.

In all the rooms of this year
I have entered one red room.

In all the futures I have walked toward
I have seen a future I can hardly name.

But here the road we drive
Turns upon another country.

I have seen white beginnings,
A slow sea without glaze or speed,
Movement of land, a long lying-down dance.

This is fog-country. Milk. Country of time.

I see your tormented color, the steep front of your storm
Break dissipated among limitless profiles.

I see the shapes of waves in the cross-sea
Advance, a fog-surface over the fog-floor.
Seamounts, slow-flowing. Color. Plunge-point of air.

In all the meanings of this year
There will be the ferny meaning.

It rises leaning and green, streams through star-lattices;
After the last cliff, wave-eroded silver,
Forgets the limitations of our love,
These drifts and caves dissolve and pillars of these countries
Long-crested dissolve to the future, a new form.

And Mama cried then, hard and sad, her back up against the blood-heavy bath, Papa's hand in hers. This was he, her dark, fire-burned man, and she had loved him, she remembered she had, and the love strong as its memory was in her veins and in his. A part of them that life had separated returned in death. The tormented colour had cleared and the limitations of their love. She remembered she had loved him and that part of herself was redeemed.

Jove and I lay on the deck boards listening to the close of the opera. Don Giovanni, unrepentant, dragged down into Hell. Do we admire him or do we despise him? Liar, cheat, murderer, seducer. As far as I know, Jove has never killed anyone. Then . . .

ME: Jove, Alice is alive, isn't she?

HE: As alive as you and I and with better odds.

ME: You didn't kill her, did you?

HE: Why would I kill Alice?

ME: To punish her. To punish me. To punish yourself.

HE: I don't believe in punishment.

ME: Of course you do. You are a Catholic.

HE: Lapsed.

ME: I noticed you had a sudden attack of faith last night.

HE: I wanted to die clean.

ME: The letter was your confession?

HE: My only confession.

ME: And all those other women?

HE: Why do you think I do it?

ME: Because you are compulsive, neurotic, infantile, selfish.

HE: Because I am alone.

ME: You are married to me.

He rolled over and sat up. He looked old, defeated.

HE: I want to go on being married to you.

ME: It's too late.

HE: Is it? If we can't live together at least we can die together.

ME: Was that the plan?

HE: No. No. A joke.

ME: My husband the graveside humorist.

He reached for the head-cans and started to work on the radio again. I went below deck to clear up the mess and to see how much food we had left. The engine and rudder had been damaged during the storm, and although we had a sail, neither of us knew how to unfurl it let alone direct it to the wind. We were drifting, sea-blasted, and our only hope was rescue. We had enough food for about four days and enough water for a week if we stopped washing. And then? I turned my mind away from then.

I got out some paper and began to write to Alice. I had the curious sensation that if I was not addressing a corpse a corpse was addressing Alice. Which of us was alive?

'My dear Alice, I do not know if or when you will receive this letter . . .' Up and above I could hear Jove cursing the indifferent circuit board. If we were officially dead, did it matter that we considered ourselves alive? To whom could we protest about this sudden re-definition? When would we come to accept it? Jove and Stella. Death by fiat.

'Will you understand? I am not sure that I understand it myself. Give me your hand. Put it to my mouth. Kiss you. Tongue, teeth, language. My words forming in bubbles under your fingers. Water and air. Hope. I want to tell you . . . and so I go diving for the words, bringing them back in glittering nets, spilled over our feet as we stand amazed at the sea. I want to tell you how . . . and so these are words speared for you, tasted for you, fed one by one. Words kept salted when they cannot be found fresh. Words kept fresh when they cannot be found clean. The words go deeper, far out of reach of vessels, blood vessels bursting, that thick humming in the head. To find the words, just out of reach, beyond my hand, the coral of it, pearl of it, fish.

Am I a pearl fisher? To crack out of the dumb the eloquent? Take this, dissolve it in wine, drink it and speak to me. Does it loosen your tongue? What marvellous things we would say if we could. What of the stories still to be told? There are Arabian Nights in your eyes. If we are in the desert, then speak the wadi. If we are in the earthquake then speak the rock. Put your hand to my mouth. Kiss me. Tongue, teeth, words. Bucket up the words and wash in them. If we are in the water speak salt tears.

I want to tell you how much . . . the expanse of us, unhindered, stretch of sea-bird wings at starboard. Stars in your eyes, the infinity of you, the galaxy of my girl that I explore. The much of you was more than I dared hope for. Treasure is the stuff of legends. Gold in the mine of you. Mine own gold. I thought you were a jewelled bird of the kind Byzantine emperors kept. Rare, fabulous, told of but unseen. What words for a plumage like yours? The surprise of wings was this love. We did escape gravity. If I flew too close to the sun, forgive me. Water claims her own at last. You were the one who understood the theory of flight. You were the one who taught me the aerodynamics of risk. I should have trusted you. The failure was mine, Alice, not the pain of having spoken and said nothing. Not the pain of words that splinter in the throat. Call every speck of me by right. Letter me. I say your name as a spell and leave my last word here as yours. I want to tell you how much I love you. You.'

I sealed it in an empty fuel canister and put it with my clothes. I wrote her name in charcoal on the tin side. There was nothing more I could do. Dry-hearted I began to cook spaghetti. Food tastes better in . . .

When Jove and I were early married we lived over the trattoria and our love-making was rhythmed to the regular whoosh and grind of the espresso machine and the thin whirr of the blade for the parma ham. Our bed was a board balanced on six huge drums of olive oil, the spaces between infilled with cartons of Signora Rossetti's pasta ready for sale. Sometimes, she or one of the boys used to come hurrying up the slanted stairs shouting '*Pasta pronto*', and it did not matter whether we were asleep or awake, in bed or out of it, the tagliatelle and the linguine had to be hauled from under our trembling mattress and dropped down the fire chute to the truck waiting below.

At least I never had to cook. Meals were taken with the rest of the extended family, eighteen of them plus two priests, all round a long table at the back of the diner. Jove had no money at all. He was without a job and his savings had gone to his divorced wife and child. I supported us by teaching German to businessmen and English literature to students who hardly knew which way up to hold a book. In the evening we both worked in the trattoria. Signora Rossetti had furious rows with her difficult son because he would use the kitchen blackboard to try out his equations. The cook, looking for the menu numbers that had been ordered, found them mixed with a set of figures that seemed to be asking her to serve sardines on top of a fried egg sauced with strawberry milkshake.

At last, Papa's dusty old attorney managed to complete the formalities of my coming-of-age bequest, and while it was not riches, it was enough to set us up in our own apartment and to free us from our chains of spaghetti.

Jove got a university job. I had time for my poetry. We were happy. I did not realise that even then he was visiting someone else. Later, he said it was because I was out all day working. Later, Signora Rossetti said to me that she was glad to be the mother of her son and not his wife. 'He'll change,' I said.

When the storm hit the boat off horizontal, and I was temporarily knocked out by a falling tilly lamp, I regained consciousness in the expectation of death. The boat would hole any minute and I would be drowned. Strangely I felt calm. There was no possibility of control or sacrifice or heroics. I was a child again at the mercy of larger forces. I clung to my bunk as Jove clung to the stove and let myself float on the wash of memories and recognitions that took the place of thinking. I did not speak to him, or hear him, although he was talking constantly, until he said Alice's name. Then I was back in my body, outside of death, hating him and wanting to live so that I could punish him for what he had done.

After many hours the storm split into two and roared off to the west and to the east, leaving us in its gap, flat and balanced again. My arms were rigid with pain. When I tried to let go of the bunk bolts I could not ungrip my fingers. Jove had to prise them open and sit me up, my arms still stretched out in front of me like a sleepwalker.

As we accustomed ourselves to this reprieve, knew ourselves again as warm and solid and breathing, we heard the bulletin on the radio. It seemed that days had passed, not dead, not alive, in the cat's paw of the storm. The irony of our livingness was that we were officially dead.

'Not quite,' said Jove. '"Presumed" has plenty of go in it yet. They'll send the choppers over when the clouds lift.'

'Nor dim nor red, like God's own head,
The glorious Sun uprist.'

I had learned Coleridge's *The Ancient Mariner* off by heart when Mama and I took the ship back to Hamburg. I had thought it was Papa following us like the albatross, the friendly bird of good omen, shot by the callous mariner. I had blamed Mama for his death. Only later could I understand a little more of their difficult love. On board ship I used to wander the deck looking for Papa as he had told me to do.

★

The clouds lifted. The sun came up, bright, rinsed. Today or the next day we would be rescued.

Rescue me. I leaned against the mocking mast furled tight as a banker's umbrella. The human condition seems to be one of waiting to be rescued. Will it be you? Will it be today? Will the world open in splendent colour, spirit-blue, that aniline blue, ripe indigo or the tone of an unclouded sky? Say it will. Each other's greatest fear. Each other's only hope. I put out my hand and withdraw it at the same time. What are my chances of choosing well? We court each other in elaborate masks and ballgowns. I clothe myself in conversation, money, wit. Whatever will win you, I become. I disguise myself as your rescuer so that you will be mine.

Self-sufficient? Or so the story goes, but two can row faster than one and I wanted to get away. So did you. Jove, Alice. Insert the name you please. Always the getaway. A new start. Rescued from the smallness that we are. My incondite life.

Perhaps Jove faces the truth better than I do: that there is no rescue. Will be none. That there are only boat rides out to sea followed by inevitable return or shipwreck. He says he is alone. He does not believe that he will be saved. He plays the game like a compulsive gambler but he does not expect to win. He says his lies are the only possible honesty. I could respect that if he had not married me.

'I had to try,' he said. 'I want to try now.'

I can tell by his desperation that in spite of his bravado he does not think that anyone will come for us. My stillness repels and fascinates him. He spends all his time fiddling with the radio or fishing or trying to rig up a make-shift rudder. Then he flops down and asks for coffee and I am serving smaller and smaller cups.

'It's my head,' I said to him, by way of explanation. When I was hit by the falling lamp I think it damaged my incudes (the bones of the middle ear). I lose my balance easily and I can hear voices. He is afraid that I am mad but I am not mad. I have been hurt and he is the hurter. I have been damaged and he has damaged me. It is easier for him to worry that I am mad.

Blame? No I don't blame him. I came here of my own free will. All the years of deceit have been of my own free will. Whatever that is.

Evening and the sky darkens to lead-blue. Morning and it begins the blue colour of skim-milk. The tough membrane that shields me from too much awareness has begun to dissolve. It is necessary to go through life a little blunted, a little cloaked, how else to bear even a single day? The horror and the glory would overwhelm me. Papa used to talk about the story of the burning bush when God appears to Moses as a roar of fire. Moses asks to see God face to face and God tells him that to do so, even partially, even for a second, would kill him with its beauty and its power. 'Who shall look on God and live?' To Papa this was the central paradox of his religion, for there is no life without God and yet to approach God means death. What Papa wanted was to widen the gateways of perception. To see as much as it was possible to see while inside the limitations of consciousness. Like all mystics he used fasting and bodily deprivation to spread out his mind while disciplining his mortal self. Some would say that his visions and his ecstasies were nothing more than physiological morbidity. I do not know, but I know that occasionally I too could look through the cleanness of him and see the kick of joy in the universe. I see something of that now, my barriers down, my defences broken. I would be afraid if

I were trying to save myself but saving myself is a thing of the past. If these are my last days then I would rather see the horror and the glory as it is.

'I am afraid,' said Jove at night-time.

We were in the bizarre circumstance of being in sight of land but unable to reach it. Without rudder or engine we could not steer ourselves, and when the tide brought us close enough to register the full outline of a series of coves and inlets, a few hours later it took us away again back to our watery blur.

The strain of this sublittoral existence was affecting Jove. He proposed that we swim for it. What if the land was barren and we were without food or water? He proposed that we use the sail. What if the wind carried us crazily away?

ME: I can't swim that far.

HE: I'll go then. I'll get help.

ME: All right. You go.

Then he wouldn't go, hesitating at the side, trying to use the angle of the sun on the mast to calculate the distance to shore.

HE: Someone must see us soon.

No one did. It was as though we had floated off the world's edge into a science-fiction sea. We saw no other craft, no aeroplanes, no sign of movement on the cruel clifftops. We had begun by tacking elegantly along a string of fishing villages overflowing with food and wine and now the storm had flung us out into a desert sea.

'How can we be nowhere?' said Jove. 'There is no nowhere left.'

'Maybe we've sailed through one of your wormholes and come up in a parallel universe. In this universe, identical to our own, there are no people.'

He turned on me in a fury. 'Stupid, stupid, stupid. The probability is beyond calculation. A large quantum transition such as that is virtually impossible.'

'Virtually?'

HE: We're at sea, in Italy, in the world, in the here and now, we're both alive and we're going to be rescued.

He kicked the radio. Its dial fell off.

'Who cares?' said Jove. 'It was squegged anyway.'

We had halved our daily water ration. We were sun-raw, windburnt, salt-swollen and dehydrated. We took it in turns to watch on deck. I sitting at the mast. Jove, cross-legged, determined, high as he could get on the cabin. We were both beginning to imagine things.

ME: If this were a film we would have to be rescued by the end.

HE: It isn't a film.

ME: No.

And back to the difficult silences.

ME: Jove, if I die and you don't will you do something for me?

HE: What?

ME: There's a diamond at the base of my spine. It belongs to the Jew you noticed at the port.

HE: What Jew?

ME: The Ashkenazi in the long coat.

HE: You mean the man in black?

ME: If I die you must cut out the diamond and give it to him.

HE: Stella . . .

He stopped. He was looking at me with that liedown/sweet tea/long sleep/nut house/make allowances look that he used as a portcullis in front of his tongue. Jove considers me mad. Does that make me mad? The authorities have declared me dead. Does that make me dead? Where is the Archimedean point? Inside? Outside? What is the proper perspective on my existence?

HE: Help me to fish?

I nodded and took the line like a garden gnome. I seem to be suffering from a kind of apraxia; an inability to perform voluntary purposeful movements. Like Papa I sit and stare at worlds visible and not.

The golden disc of the sun and the wave-curve. Sun like a disc-saw cutting the blue sheets of the sea. The sun-cut sea carrying the boat. The boat serene with its ragged crew.

Jumping fish escort us and crying birds watch overhead. At

night, our white deck in the black space makes a landing pad for the moon. Moonlight in the portholes and in washes on our bunks. We lie under it, eyes like craters, moon-filled.

La Lune. Card XVIII of the Tarot. A mysterious light over an eremic landscape two dogs howl upwards. Below, a crayfish, ancient, armoured, lifts its claws from a blue pool.

'We are lost, Jove.'

'Not yet. Don't say it yet.'

HE: Do you remember the first man on the moon?

ME: We were in Vermont.

HE: No clock only the oak spreading over the evening.

ME: That oak must have been two hundred years old.

HE: You said, 'It will live for two hundred years more. Why should we hurry?'

ME: We had been making love in the dirt since the Declaration of Independence.

HE: Wars and Empire and the passing of Empire had not disturbed us.

ME: It was as if we had made love always and always would.

HE: We rolled over to look at the astronaut, stepping clumsily in his dumb-bell suit, picking up rocks for NASA.

ME: It was history.

HE: You were naked and the night was cool.

ME: It was a long way to fly for a rock.

We were in our separate bunks, his hand over the side towards me, his familiar arm, solid as an anchor. His voice a harbour.

HE: History has no smell.

ME: Is that why we are nostalgic for it?

HE: Breathe in, breathe out. The past doesn't stink like the present.

ME: Were we happier or do we pretend?

HE: We pretend.

ME: You said it was my smell you loved.

HE: The hidden world of pheromones.

ME: This armpit seducer.

HE: This armchair Don Juan.

ME: Your mother had truffles from the forests outside Rome. They smelled of earth and roots and sweat.

HE: They use a machine now for rootling truffles.

ME: A pig is pork.

HE: They use a machine now for matching couples.

ME: Love is money.

HE: I don't know what love is.

ME: You never waited long enough to find out.

HE: Patience isn't a vice of mine.

ME: Not all experiments yield their results in a single night.

HE: Why do you confuse love and sex?

ME: Why do you continually separate them?

HE: Are we going to spend our last hours arguing?

ME: Yes.

He laughed and swung off the bunk and knelt down by my head. In the moonlight I might have mistaken him for a knight in shining armour. His T-shirt was neon-lit. He had grown a beard, or to be fairer, a beard had grown over his face. His eyes and teeth were wolfish. He was emblematic of safety and threat as knights in shining armour are. The drama of the rescue conceals its implications.

HE: There isn't anything to eat.

ME: No.

HE: Would you like to eat me?

ME: What?

HE: I'm sure there are certain parts of me you wouldn't object to lopping off.

ME: Stop this.

HE: No, seriously, what's it to be? Die with both legs, survive with one? How much of me could we eat and still say that I am alive? Arms. Legs. Slices of rump. Your grandfather was a butcher. Try me.

He reached over for the curved filleting knife, gave it to me, and raised his bottom into the air. The sight of him, jacked over under the moon, made me start to laugh, quietly at first, then as the pain in my head increased, louder, and harsher. He started to laugh too, a pair of jackals we were, crouched and baying at the moon.

The boat was still, hardly rocking at all. Stumbling together, we half fell, half climbed, up the steps to the deck. He gripped me, his prick straight in, the swollen saltiness of it dirty in my dirt. I was dry and cracked, unwashed, closed. I had a weeping rash on my inner thighs.

I held onto him, holding onto the years in between, the years notched in his back, his vertebral column, twenty-four separate, moving irregular bones, the years of our life together.

When the push of him stopped we were both still. He rested his head in the cradle of my shoulder and I felt him crying. Not the salt sea but these few tears capsized what hope remained. I thought of Alice's hand, her long thin fingers like leaf-nerves. I thought of the leaves falling on my back when I had made love in Vermont. Or had that been Alice? Or had it been Jove?

Fragments of coloured glass, radiating fanwise, a diadrom of feeling spreading out through my mind, its life-jacket lost. The reassuring buoying padded stuff that floated me and insulated me has been ripped away. I am exposed now, and my discriminating, differentiating functions are useless tools in this unmoored sea. Where is the beginning? Where is the end? Where is the horizon? Where is the land? The moon swings down on me like a hook. The boat is a blade, knife-edge of consciousness precarious on the unconscious sea. Whatever it is, it is deeper. Whatever it is, it is unfathomable. The point that I am, the definite bounded thing in time, is beginning to break up. I am dispersing myself through my known past and my unknown future. The present is without meaning.

Does it live? Does it all live? I know that other worlds are lost to me as surely as I am lost to other worlds. I know that what I am is clouded, refractory, partial. That to a lightwave I am already dead, my small circuit of time entirely belted by his, His? Shall I call him Lucifer, Lord of the Lightwaves? *Vite, Vite*, to God's steady tread?

Cast up in a body, I find the long past of me like a fossil in stone. What was it that moved so determinedly, and slunk at last into bas-relief? The fern is preserved but it will not grow. The creature in its coildom is safe and safe it stays. What risk? And without risk what movement? Better that I release my bones into these waves than lie still in this body of stone. It is too heavy for me now. What matters is outside it. I cannot at will raise an arm or a leg. The patient fuse of my pain has burned down. My head is a firework display. The sense of who I am is strengthening and weakening simultaneously. Papa said, 'Learn to remember your real face.' He never looked in a mirror. Is that him rowing towards me, his dark figure upright in a moon-scooped boat?

Papa! Papa! Yes, he has seen me. In a moment he will be here.

Alice. My voice over the water, skimming in a bright curve to where she is. What distance? What measure? Nothing that separates us but a moment's thought. Dear girl, there is so much to say. Words unbottled splashing over our feet. Did you get my message, thrown out to sea, my message to you that we are a single, clear happiness?

How simple it is now. I seem to be tumbling over myself, ready to tunnel out of the womb of the world, my hands and feet bouncing off its warm wall.

On the night I was born the sky was punched with stars. Diamonds deep in the earth's crust. Diamonds deep in the stellar wall. As above, so below. Uniting carbon mediated in my gem-stole body. When a baby is born, its anterior fontanelle, at the back of the skull and diamond-shaped, is the last of the sutures to close. Resisting ossification, it is an eloquent wound. What has been, what will be, star-dust that we are. Uniquely the carrier of history, this vulnerable human cell, cosmos-hurled.

KNAVE OF COINS

I had to do it. She was dead. She was nearly dead or I would not have done it. If I had not done it she would have died anyway. I did it because I had to. What else could I have done?

It was after the storm that she began to complain of headaches and dizziness. The unnatural calm of the sea, our Neptunian isolation, seemed focused and magnified in her behaviour. While I tried to do everything I could to save us, she sat in Buddha-calm against the mast. Psychologists call it *abaissement du niveau mental*. It was as though she had been overpowered.

By what? There is a history of psychosis in my wife's family. Her father was a crank. He built for himself a shuttered world, out of touch with reality, dangerously divorced from the hit and miss of humankind. As a young man, like any other young man, I used to visit the meat-houses around Times Square. The girls were clean and cheap and it was a process of initiation. My pals and I talked politics while we were waiting our turn. It was the mid-Fifties. There had been a lot of unrest. At least late-night shagging was not considered to be an un-American activity.

I used to see my wife's father, crossing Times Square in the dead of night, carpet bag in hand like a dealer. He talked to himself, sometimes slamming to a stop for no reason, never noticing anyone else. He used to drag his little girl around with him.

He and the mother lived in separate rooms in their apartment. Most of the time he stayed at the bookstore he kept for a living. Even the windows seemed to repel the light.

My wife's mother had an affair with an Englishman brought over to run a shipping sideline. I think his name was Pinkerton. Maybe not. When he left for his real wife back home, Uta had a breakdown. Soon after that, the Jew, the wild man, her husband Ishmael, killed himself. I never found out how. Or maybe I have forgotten.

Mother and child returned to Berlin. Nine years later, when Stella came back to New York she walked into our family business carrying a Bowie knife. I had to disarm her. She was fragile, gentle, wide awake in a sleeping world. I was attracted to her energy without realising that it was a kind of craziness. Her father had been magnetic too. I used to follow him all night sometimes. Why did I do that?

I thought that if Stella lived with me and my family in a normal family way that she might regain the equilibrium she needed. After all, she was born on a sledge.

All of us have fantasies, dreams. A healthy society outlets those things into sport, hero-worship, harmless adultery, rock climbing, the movies. Unhealthy individuals understand their dreams and fantasies as something solid. An alternative world. They do not know how to subordinate their disruptive elements to a regulated order. My wife believed that she had a kind of interior universe as valid and as necessary as her day-to-day existence in reality. This failure to make a hierarchy, this failure to recognise the primacy of fact, justified her increasingly subjective responses. She refused to make a clear distinction between inner and outer. She had no sure grasp either of herself or of herself in relation to the object. At first I mistook this pathology as the ordinary feminine.

I had to do it. She was dead. She was nearly dead or I would not have done it. If I had not done it she would have died anyway. I did it because I had to. What else could I have done?

I am in sympathy with an organic view of nature; a symbiotic participating structure that in no way resembles Newton's Mechanics. Every day my work surprises me and I am sceptical of theories that seem to point to truth but just don't fit the facts. Physics cannot rig the evidence, either it is honest science or it is not science at all. Call it alchemy, astrology, spoon-bending, wishful thinking. All of which my wife enjoyed, along with a mystical disposition that sadly, some of my colleagues share. There is nothing mystical about the universe. There are things we cannot explain yet. That is all.

Matter is energy. Of course. But for all practical purposes matter is matter. Don't take my word for it. Bang your head against a brick wall. The shifting multiple realities of quantum physics are real enough but not at a level where they affect our lives. I deal in them every day and I, like you, still have to wash my underpants. In a parallel universe somewhere near here I may never have to wash my underpants, but until then, no mystical union with the One will muffle the stink.

SHE: Why not join the Flat Earth Club?

HE: The earth is not flat.

SHE: For all practical purposes it is.

HE: Not all.

SHE: For my purposes a single objective reality will not do.

HE: You still have to wash your underpants.

SHE: How about joining the Flat Brain Club?

Stella, wide awake in a sleeping world, never understood that it is better to let sleeping dogs lie. The world is not ready to wake up yet. The world is still sleeping in its coverlet of stars. I touched her face, her eyelids fluttering, tears under them, where the pain was. No more crying. No more pain. I would be tender as the night that covers up your foolishness and mine. The world is real and it has hurt us. Signs, shadows, wonders, do you still believe that, now that your multiple world has hardened into this brick wall?

She had banged her head. The blow had concussed her. Poseidon-lost on our lonely sea, she would not let me swim for help. She would not try to fish. When the water was gone I survived by draining the engine. There were a few pints of oily fluid in there. Just enough to near poison me and to save my life. If only she had been stronger. Just a few days stronger.

★

I had to do it. She was dead. She was nearly dead or I would not have done it. If I had not done it she would have died anyway. I did it because I had to. What else could I have done?

She had been talking about the diamond. When we were first married she told me the story of her gem-besotted mother, which I can believe because Uta loved jewels. I can even believe the swallowing and the retrieval but I cannot accept that Stella had a precious stone in her hip. She showed me an X-ray, and sure enough there is a pea-like thing in there but it looks like shot to me; an air-rifle peppering from a gun-loose kid. I talked to a couple of doctors about the story and they both confirmed that it was impossible. I don't mind my wife telling me stories. I worry when she can no longer distinguish between the fanciful and the actual.

Perhaps it was a mistake to write to her about Alice. That is, to write as though Alice were writing. To reveal an affair. To shock her. I wanted to bring her to her senses.

When she took up the game, though I suppose it wasn't a game to her, I was surprised, excited. I wanted to find out what would happen next.

A threesome? I suppose so. I wanted to see them together, myself as the invisible other. I watched them in the bar, followed them to the diner, walked behind them to the Battery, saw them in to my own apartment. Imagined what they would do. Oddly, I never thought that they would really *do* anything, the sex was a surprise. I made the mistake of thinking that I could control the experiment. I won't make that mistake again. This time it nearly cost me my life.

Yes, my life. You are what you eat. There was nothing to eat. I kept slipping backwards in my mind to the night with Alice when she confessed that she would like to do it with a woman. We were eating liver. Liver. I couldn't get my mind off the liver. When Stella and I finished the last of the cheese biscuits I was salivating liver. I'm sure you know it is the largest internal organ in the body weighing between two and five pounds. When I looked at Stella what I saw was her liver.

I had to do it. She was dead. She was nearly dead or I could not have done it. If I had not done it she would have died anyway. I did it because I had to. What else could I have done?

We had made love. We were close that night. We had talked and argued as we always did. Stella's people are genetically engineered to dispute. Even their god, Jehovah, passes most of the Old Testament in dispute with someone, often Himself. My people are as many-shooted as our grape vines. We have our own opinions and we change them if we want to. What flourishes today may be clipped off tomorrow. Until then, nothing else is. So Stella and I argued. It was our intimacy.

We had made love. I had been joking with her. Her old self surfaced in flashes, then the sea took it, and she was out of my depth again. She asked me to give the Jew the diamond. I wanted her to shut up. That kind of talk frightened me and I was scared enough by then. When she said we might have slipped through a kink in time, I almost, almost, started to believe her. Our isolation was uncanny. It felt as though we had sailed off the sea and into the stars themselves. I kept my sanity by making little cuts in my arm with a filleting knife. As long as it hurt I was real, I was alive. 'I think therefore I am' had no meaning anymore. Quite often I had the disagreeable sensation that I was being thought. This is a common effect of attenuation.

The night was cool and silent. The moon was bladed. The wash of the sea on the boat had the sound of my mother's ham slicer, the swish, swish of the keen edge through the easy pink. I fell into a kind of dream, almost a trance, a hunger trance, I suppose, and I was a child again and my mother was feeding me. There was a plate of fresh olives and bread, and swish, swish, she was slicing the ham onto my plate. Uta loved ham. She used to come to us on Saturdays, the Jewish Shabbat, and eat platefuls of forbidden pig. Stella always refused and her Mama had to buy her spaghetti. Little Stella, eating the pale strings one by one. Uta, mouth open, a contrast to her prettiness and delicacy, every finer sense brought beneath her cured idol. When she had finished her course of parma ham, she ordered liver and onions.

I woke up. I could smell liver. I half rose over Stella's body. She was talking, what was she saying? It was something about the diamond again. I said *Stop it stop it*, but it was as if she couldn't hear me, as if my voice, high and cracked, was snatched upwards, while she, lying still, aimed her words at my empty belly, each one a punch.

I wanted her to be quiet, that was all, for both our sakes, and I must have picked her up, doll-like-dead as she was, still talking, and I must have dropped her head against the swollen splitting planks, or was it her head that was swollen and splitting? I said *Stop it stop it*.

Then she was quiet.

I made the cut so carefully. I made it like a surgeon not a butcher. My knife was sharp as a laser. I did it with dignity, hungry though

I was. I did it so that it would not have disgusted either of us. She was my wife. I was her husband. We were one flesh. With my body I thee worship. In sickness and in health. For better or for worse. Till death us do part. Till death us do part.

I parted the flesh from the bone and I ate it.

I had to do it. She was dead. She was nearly dead or I would not have done it. If I had not done it she would have died anyway. I did it because I had to. What else could I have done?

THE LOVERS

My mother and I were aboard the *QE2*. A spring cruise of fun and fantasy where every day had been parcelled and labelled with a mortician's care. There was an undertaker on board but his services were not usually required.

My mother had been intending to travel with my father to Hong Kong. It had been part of his retirement package, now guiltily extended over sea miles, calendar months and attendant family members.

I had agreed to accompany my mother to Cherbourg, Capri, and as far as New York. On board ship, after I had put her to bed with a sedative, I had gone to the bridge to visit Captain Ahab, my father's friend, my childhood adventurer. While I was waiting for him, I idly read the maritime bulletins.

★

MISSING PRESUMED DEAD

A yacht sailing off Capri was last sighted on Sunday June 16 at 18:00 hours. The boat was in difficulties. Severe storms prevented rescue attempts for 24 hours. It is thought that the boat could be drifting at sea.

It was a hoax. It had to be a hoax. My thoughts, such as they were, my panics, my suspicions, my hatred, blew easterly and blew sour. Wherever they were, they would be safe, moored in their love. They had known that my father was dying and they had abandoned me.

MISSING PRESUMED DEAD . . . Not true. Not true. Impossible that she should be dead. My gut was still connected to her. The present was not cut off from the future, emptied of blood. It was not Stella who was dead, not Stella and Jove, playing the games of the living. It was my father, my father who was dead. My father who was dead. Repeat it. Repeat it. Would the dead pile on the dead in an open grave?

Here is the Captain. He will tell me the truth. The Captain, my father's age, my father's build, as kindly and dependable as the sea underneath him was not. No more tricks. No more lies. He would tell me the truth.

As I embraced him I thought, 'Suicide pact?' Jove, who loved a flamboyant ending, Stella, who could not fail to be seduced by one. Jove, unstable as uranium. Stella, a living fission.

And I? Closed off behind lead shutters; heavy, soft, blue-grey unhappiness dumbing me.

I told Captain Ahab about my relationship with Jove. I did not tell him about my relationship with Stella.

★

In London, before my mother and I had left for our Southampton tide, I had gone into my father's room and opened his top drawer. The handkerchiefs were there, gaudy, luxuriant, waiting their turn for display. His watch was among them, silent now, no more quarters to the hour.

I had sat on the floor, sieving the silk through my fingers, the weight, the smoothness, thinking about him. Deep in the drawer out of easy reach, I had found a bundle of letters, each envelope postmarked Berlin, the packet held together by the remains of a red silk tie. I looked at the signatures.

'Your loving Uta.'

'Never tell all thy love.' My father in the Algonquin Hotel fastening his collar with a woman's red-silk memory.

I am my father's daughter.

The Captain promised me that he would find out all he could. I walked back to my cabin with a faint mixture of resignation and hope. Faint because nothing seemed able to penetrate my numbness. The sump of me was full already. The pain had nowhere to drain away and I could not hold any more. New pain did not, as yet, mean more pain. There was pain and I was airless under it.

I kept thinking back to the Algonquin Hotel. Myself with my father in his tie, myself with Stella, dressed against hurt. As I half slept, I could not fully distinguish which was my father/myself, Stella/Uta, whether the distance we imagine separates one event from another had folded up, leaving the two clock faces to slide together, plates of time, synchronous.

Look at the sun. The sun you see is eight minutes in the past, the time it takes for light to travel the distance between the sun's eye and yours.

Look at the galaxy. What you see is thousands, sometimes tens of thousands of years past, drama of the nebula only visible when it reaches us, effort of light, 186,000 miles per second, crossing centuries of history, still dark to us. The distances are vast. Space and time become space-time.

How long does it take for an event to reach me? I thought I was present, thought I understood it all, but only later, in the cliché of a blinding light, do I realise the significance of what happened. Only in the present do I begin to recognise my own past.

'Look at me.' Jove standing behind me on this ship in a ship's mirror, his mouth, a pair of scissors cutting through my resolve. I had turned from the mirror image to look at him and he had kissed me. I closed my eyes, one does, perhaps that is why it took so long for light from the event to reach me. I begin to see what it was I did.

As I waited, no word, I began to play a macabre game. If only one of them were alive, which one would I hope for? Champion Jove? Winning Stella? Which one of them did I love beyond the greedy love that we all shared? There was a bitterness to this dreadful game because I guessed that neither of them had chosen me.

Last month, after our moot, Stella showed me Card XVI of the Tarot deck, L'amoureux, The Lovers. A young man seems to be trying to choose between two women, Cupid, arrow-borne, over his head.

SHE: The Eternal Triangle.

ME: Three is a masculine number. Odd numbers are masculine.

SHE: Or are masculine numbers odd?

ME: It's my fault.

SHE: It's all our fault.

She looked at the picture. 'I think, perhaps, that the women are trying to decide for themselves and the man is taking no notice.'

ME: How do you feel?

SHE: Stop thinking of feeling as something you have to hunt down.

ME: I am much better at saying how I feel when I no longer feel it.

SHE: The dead bury the dead?

ME: I didn't mean . . .

SHE: I know. I have made up my mind.

ME: What?

SHE: It is my own decision. Not for Jove and not for you. For myself. That is the only proper way to begin again.

I never found out what it was she had decided. She had arranged to meet me the following day but I had the telephone call from my mother and I have not seen Stella since then.

In the night, dream-disturbed, I was swimming breast stroke in a black sky, no light in it. I turned over onto my back, and kicking with my feet to keep myself level, I saw the stars in an upturned hod, tipping out over me. I raised my arm to shield my face.

'Stella! Stella!' Who touched me? I awoke on the silent ship. Two thousand five hundred souls, and I, alone.

In the early morning, the sky mosaiced with birds, I heard from the Captain that the yacht was our yacht, that a thorough search had revealed nothing, no wreckage, no bodies, no impedimenta, no signal. The waters were dotted with fishing boats and cruisers. The yacht could not have disappeared but it had disappeared.

As a star collapses, the force of gravity on its surface becomes stronger, and because light beams bend under gravity, the space-time around the star becomes more and more curved. Eventually the star reaches a stage where nothing, not even light, can get away from it. An event horizon forms around the star, preventing any signal reaching the worlds outside. We know where it should be but we shall never see it. Its light is trapped.

I went to Captain Ahab and asked him to send me in one of the launches, straight away to Capri. It was an absurd request and he agreed, even though he had to swing his ship slightly off course to land me at the little port I needed. And so, in the middle of the sea, at dawn, I acted as a human remora, smaller than small, bigger than big, attaching myself to the rudder of the world's largest liner and fixing its way.

It was now eight days since Jove and Stella had gone missing.

At the hotel reception there was a note for me.

'You must have the wrong person. No one is expecting me here.'

'*No, no, Signora, questo e il vostro nome.*'

I opened the faded envelope. The instructions, in ink, were clear. Hire a boat. Meet the writer at the quay at tide.

Why did I do it? There was no other way forward and it was too late to turn back.

The Ship of Fools will be sailing tonight.

On board: Captain Alluvia Fairfax. A cabin boy who speaks no English and wears a tag around his neck that reads 'Friday'. The third, a gentleman who stood behind me as I roped the boat and said, 'Call me Ishmael.'

I swung round to him. His skin looked as if it had been stretched over his body with tongs. He was piano-wire taut. The wound tension in him vibrated. He was still and not still. He had been pitched at A flat. When he spoke his voice held a curious tremolo.

He was dressed in black. His shoes were dusty. His trousers hung as though they had some time since devoured his legs. His white shirt had yellowed to ivory. His waistcoat was high cut, George the Third English, of what had been an expensive material. Now it had retreated into black holes of self-oblivion. He wore no tie. His coat, to the floor, had a bag of bread rolls in one vast pocket. His hat had been the patient receiver of a lifetime of knocks. He took off his hat when he spoke to me. His hair, falling over his face, had no grey in it. I had once peered into the crater of a volcano and seen its lava, hot and remote. Such were his eyes.

His manner was gentle. He held his hat like a shield over his navel while he talked. His voice was quiet and unambiguous. Friday sat on the deck in the lolling water and stared and stared at this upright figure of insistence.

'I will take you to them, my *liebling* and the *k'nacker*.'

'Why haven't you told anyone what you know?'

'I was waiting for you.'

'You didn't know I was coming.'

He shrugged and gestured towards the boat *'Ich eil zich.'*

Cast off, we curved over the sea, star-reflected.

I prayed that Jove and Stella would be alive. Why had I agreed to the holiday? I had been reluctant to do so. It was Jove who had persuaded me how much the holiday would mean to Stella. I wanted her to be happy. I did not want my own feelings to capsize us.

My feelings dismay me. I so rarely control them. They are their own kingdom, too primitive to be a republic, and when they want to, they send their armies to batter me. My total self should include feeling but I do not know how to make a treaty with that warrior state. When I was growing up I rebelled against feeling and now my feelings rebel against me.

I separated myself from too much hurt. Even now, there is a close association in my gut between feeling and pain. Logically I recognise that feeling is, often is, pleasure and delight. Nevertheless, at an instinctual level, at a level outside of logic, feeling is pain.

I love badly. That is, too little or too much. I throw myself over an unsuitable cliff, only to reel back in horror from a simple view out of the window. The melodrama of my childhood has located itself in a heroes/villains psyche of He Loves Me He Loves Me Not. The lecherous twirling moustaches, the asexual saintly fore-head, my lovers divided into exciting predators and insipid prey.

In this overlit twilight world, the fluorescent compensating for the lack of natural light, my feelings run riot on sadism, masochism, ruthlessness and mutilation. Exactly what you would expect from a barbarian state. I am civilised. My feelings are not.

I want to love well. To see you as you are, not as a character in my film noir. I want the unknowableness and intimacy of another human being.

I say I appear naked before you, but so often I whistle for my invisible armed guard; the gap-toothed, jeering, club-headed mob, my feelings, that are used to having me to themselves.

At my mother and father's *foie gras* parties, I invented for myself a squat-faced troll who pulped the hated guests with a nailed bat. This troll, Anger, his crony Pain, were easier to summon than to banish. As I grew older, they mated, and now I have a squadron as Snow White had her Seven Dwarfs. Anger, Pain, Fearful, Nervy, Callous, Nightmare and Ruthless. Keepers of my soft heart, they feed upon it. How shall I coax them to leave off their meat and come blinking upwards into the light?

When I met Jove there was a brief burst of liberation. Then my unconscious watchers reclaimed the land. Old habits twisted round new chances. If I had a squadron he kept a battalion. He had one virtue; he did not call sex, love.

When I met Stella, I was so excited and appalled at making love to another woman that the Miseries took much longer to regroup. Old patterns of behaviour could not be re-established because I had never known anything like this before. The shock of the new and it worked.

For a time. Then the trolls wiped that look of amazement off their vestigial faces and came at me again, Nervy and Fearful in the lead.

I did something extraordinary. That is, extraordinary for me. As they were punching Stella to death, using my voice, my arguments, my cleverness brutally turned to their account, I pulled her out of the way and stood in between. My lover was not my enemy. They were.

If this is going to succeed it will take years. I will have to find the years because I want to stand before you naked. I want to love you well.

Out now, into the willing water. The sum of all possible universes is here, now, at this prow, at this mast. Our sea co-ordinates plot our venturing point, but our wave function describes where we are and where we are not. Glancing at Ishmael as he eats his stew, I would not swear an affidavit that he is here and nowhere else. His body itself stretches. He is more of a constellation than a man. Here's his belt, his arm, his leg, his mind, who knows? The parts of him are star-flung.

I used to argue with Jove about wave functions. What to him were manipulatable facts were for me imaginative fictions. Experimentally, it is beyond doubt that electrons exhibit contrary and simultaneous behaviour. What does that suggest about us? About our reality? What is unwritten draws me on, the difficulty, the dream.

We cannot talk about atoms anymore because 'atom' means indivisible. We have split it.

Can we talk about reality anymore when reality means 'that which actually exists. Not counterfeit or assumed.' What does actually exist? The universe has become a rebus.

I touch you and you disappear. Always you escape me. The nearer I come to you the further off you seem. The more I know of you the more enigmatical you are. *Cogito ergo sum* or is it *Amo ergo sum*? I think therefore I am? I love therefore I am? What has defined me at the clearest point of my out-spread life has been my love for you. Not a raft or a lifebelt. A fix in the flux.

Matter is provisional and that includes me. Matter has at best a tendency to exist, and will, it seems, divide infinitely because there is no there there. There are vibrations, relationships, possibilities and out of these is formed our real life.

Still and still moving matter. String paradox of the restless and the formed. If the physics is correct then we are neither alive nor dead as we commonly understand it, but in different states of potentiality.

Absurd? Yes. I know it is absurd. I have buried my father. While we were at the graveside, the priest intoning, my grandmother whispering to herself, over and over, 'David is in heaven now, David is in heaven now,' my mind was repeating Schrödinger's Cat, Schrödinger's Cat.

The Schrödinger Cat experiment. The new physics belch at the politely seated dinner table of common sense. An imaginary cat is put in a box with a gun at its head. The gun is connected to a geiger counter. The geiger counter is triggered to a piece of uranium. Uranium molecules are unstable. If the uranium decays, the process will alert the geiger counter, which in turn will cause the gun to fire. So much for the precarious fate of the Virtual cat. To observe the cat's fate we will have to open the box, but what is the state of the cat before we open the box? According to the mathematics of its wave function, it is neither alive nor dead. The wave function describes the sum of all possible states of the cat. Until a measurement is made we can't actually know the state of the particle. The cat, like it or not, is a series of particles. It shares the potentiality of the entire universe. It is finite and infinite, dead and alive. It is a quantum cat.

Absurd? Yes. Einstein, who could not refute the mathematics or deny the evidence of the experiments, hated the conclusion. What kind of a conclusion is it? The truth is, we don't know. As yet, the cat has outwitted us.

Open the box? Not me. I will see what I expect to see, the cat either dead or alive. I cannot see past my three-dimensional concept of reality, bound as it is to good/bad, black/white, real/unreal, alive/dead. Mathematics and physics, as religion used to do, form a gateway into higher alternatives, a reality that can be apprehended but not perceived. A reality at odds with common sense. The earth is not flat.

'What you see is not what you think you see.'

'Pardon me?'

'Shadows, signs, wonders.'

'Who are you?'

There was no answer, or if there was an answer it was drowned out by our cabin boy shouting, 'Friday! Friday! Friday!' We had been sailing for about nine hours. It was the morning of the next day.

Friday had sighted the boat, about a half hour away, listing badly, no radio communication. I swung the wheel so rapidly that I broke my finger. I did not notice till later. When my father died I had not seen him for two years. Until I sat by his bedside there was a distance of two years between us, a long way to cross, and news of his condition had been like glass breaking far away. Now the glass was breaking round my head. His death and theirs.

We manoeuvred alongside and I jumped the gap shouting at Friday to hold us steady. Stella was lying on the deck, her eyes closed, her body in a pool of blood. Very gently I turned the dead weight of her. My heart came up into my mouth and I vomited. Her buttock and her hip had been chopped away.

There was a noise from below. I don't know what I expected. Jove dragged himself up out of the cabin, his upper lip and chin bearded with blood. In his hand he had a filleting knife. He saw me, terror, horror, unbelief, relief, and fainted.

Like one who sleeps I radioed for a rescue helicopter. Ishmael was kneeling over Stella, his face close to hers, he was keening or making a noise like a recheat, a horn-call into the wilderness of his grief. He had his hand on her wounded thigh and the sun on his hand made a poultice of light. He held up something, put it in his mouth, cleaned it with spittle. He took it out and rubbed it over Stella's eyes and face. It was articulate with light. With his fingers he opened her mouth and laid the diamond onto her tongue.

'Papa?'

She was alive.

Jove and Stella were air-lifted off the damaged yacht. I had no choice but to sail my boat back to port with Friday and Ishmael. The roof of the sky was low. Our mast seemed to graze through the electric stars like a trolley-bus wire. We sped.

ME: Who are you?

HE: A temporary imprint in a temporary place . . . Since the beginning of time you and I have been sitting here, talking, listening, sliding the bottle between us, but it was not us, or it was some other us, marked out, firm for a moment, fading, disappearing, replacing ourselves.

The air is thick with dead bodies. Breathe in, breathe out the daily crematorium. Lung up on the dead. The bellows in your rib cage are home to millions, tall like you, uncertain like you, mother, father, sister, friend, tenemented into spinning lots, decayed from mastery into breath.

You live on particle physics. You are a science museum.

What tales would they tell, those compressed mites whom neither name nor influence nor jewels nor obscurity can save from the merciless vacuum of your nostrils? What do you not know that there is in you now, a Caesar, a Raphael, a tear of Mozart, the ended bowel problems of Napoleon at Waterloo? Breathe, all powerful one, and vanquish kingdoms as you do. Your idiot nose has sucked up Rome. Your open mouth has spewed out the Thames.

What Rome? What Thames? The flaking stone, the crumbles of bread, the dirt on the feet of St Peter, the patina of the Basilica, petals from Easter Sunday 1603, the drift of barges, tar of warships, twists of sheep wool, quick of eel. The tallow, felt, oil, food, intestinal belch of matter breaking down, breaking up, passing on, passing into you, star-dust that you are, dust to dust.

The dead are laughing at last. Hold your nose, and you become them, sinking airless to the tomb. Dive your lungs with clean, fresh air and you must feed upon their plankton, whale-like.

Call you Pantagruel? What Fe Fi Fo Fum do the

giants plan? Call yourself a lady, taking fingers and toes like snuff? The circuits of your air are a nightmare out of Bosch. Potentates and pig farmers fertilise your nasal scrub. Call yourself upright, uncorrupted, when your very life depends on history's compost?

Sneeze? After all I have told you, you are going to sneeze? Call yourself Vesuvius? Your larval eruptions have shattered the room into a Pompeii of time's wreckage. You have strewn the table-top with palaces.

Ashes to ashes, dust to dust, breath to breath.

'And the Lord God scooped up the clay of the earth and made of it a manikin and breathed into it His own breath . . .'

Breathe in, breathe out.

The wind bloweth where it listeth, throwing in your face a harvest of peasant women from the Ukraine. Broken snowfall of winter 1947. A piece of glass from the Empire State. You are what you breathe.

You dream what you breathe. Images, that in daylight float random and strange, coalesce in the untutored night when the particle world becomes you.

The dead live again. The destroyed are rebuilt. There is music, dancing, food unfound in recipe books. Your body refleshes the air. You are still the perfect clay, amiable, vital, capable of being breathed upon and accepting that breath as your own.

Those scents are images. The perfumer's art is yours. You decode the air into its own language. The pyramids belong to you and the ark on many waters. Men and women crowd at your command. A single clover idly picked breathes you back to that summer when . . .

Breathe in, breathe out. You breathe time and time's decay. Matter disposing of itself, still imprinted with its echo, the form it took, the shape of its energy for a little while.

The mediaevals thought that the damned lived in Satan's belly, hot pouch of indigestion, but damned or saved, what we were continues in the lungs of each other. Nitrogen, oxygen, tell-tale carbon.

Do not mistake me. This is not the afterlife. This is no after life. There is life, constantly escaping from the forms it inhabits, leaving behind its shell. Ashes to ashes, dust to dust. History is in your nostrils.

ME: Who are you?

HE: Look in the mirror, Alice, who are you? What table rappers we are, summoning each other across ethers of common sense.

ME: We have never met.

HE: What we are doing does not exist.

ME: This intimacy of thin air.

HE: Is it so hard to believe?

ME: Truth is found in odd places.

HE: Everything possible to be believed is an image of truth.

ME: Who are you?

The port. Bustle, fish, nets of spider-crab, a lorry unloading crates of aqua minerale and vino frizzante, fasces of grissini piled outside the harbour trattoria, broad red and white stripes of the awning, jacinth and amber of fish in the ornamental tank, brooding blue of the claw-bound lobster on the crushed ice.

Children and men were hauling and jumping, shouting commands across the high masts and wet stones. Here and there, the swank of a motor launch, impatient blare of testosterone, jostling for an opening in the crowded harbour.

The women were standing in groups, checking off the merchandise as it was dragged up from the holds, dropped down from the trucks. The men, legs apart, arms akimbo, noisily denied all knowledge of shortages and breakages, while the women waved printed-up order sheets and shrilled a flight of abuse over the static 'No, no, no' of the delivery men. Sea-birds and cats fought over the garbage.

The benign sun. The open sky. The sea as innocent as a baby's bath. Tang of salt, smell of rosemary, artichokes and cep drifting the air with wholesome rot. Outside the booths, the geraniums, red in terracotta, were flares of early summer. A boy came by eating pepper pizza. I felt a simple clean sensation. I was hungry.

As I guided my boat into the hire bay, I saw the *carabinieri*. Of course. Friday had leapt ashore and was expertly securing us to the water-pole. I turned to Ishmael. He had gone.

I would have to explain my peregrinations and copula alone.

Since the truth would certainly be written off as an unfact I decided to lie. The most plausible explanations usually are lies. What do you say to others about yourself? In any case, in a police cell, the earth is still flat.

JUDGEMENT

Walk with me.

At this point in the story I can say only what happened: that Stella had plastic surgery. That she always will walk with a slight limp.

That Jove was able to avoid criminal charges on the grounds of temporary insanity.

'Temporary all his life,' said Stella.

I visited them both in hospital. He, surrounded by Italian nurses listening to his extraordinary story of survival, which did not include eating his wife. She, reflective in a room without mirrors, sun at her head and feet.

SHE: I had decided to divorce Jove before he took a bite out of me.

ME: Will you stop it? He could have killed you.

SHE: Victim or volunteer?

ME: He lied to you.

SHE: He is a liar.

ME: And that forgives him?

SHE: I forgive him.

ME: What?

SHE: And I forgive you.

ME: I don't understand.

SHE: Shouldn't I forgive the woman who first took my husband and then took his wife?

ME: You took me. Both of you.

SHE: Victim or volunteer?

ME: Accomplice?

SHE: Rights begin where love ends. Shall we argue over who is the most to blame?

ME: He could have killed you.

SHE: This year, last year, any year. I am the one who has to say 'Stop'.

ME: Does that mean me?

SHE: Does it?

★

216

She put her finger to my lips.

SHE: This is not the time.

Summer curved into autumn and Stella came back to New York. We went to see Abel Glinert, whose family have followed Stella since she was a child. He had not been at the port. He had lost track of his inherited quarry when she had left for Italy. We took the diamond to him, and he held it up, confident in the light. I thought I too was in the red kitchen on that snowy night when Uta had escaped and seen her soul skimming towards her across the impassive sea.

Her soul? Stella's? The Jews believe that the soul comes to inhabit the body at the moment of birth. Until then, until the image of itself becomes flesh, it pursues its crystal pattern, untied. Wave function of life scattered down to one dear face. How else can I know you but through the body you rent? Forgive me if I love it too much.

What was it Uta saw? Uta, down at the water, First Class, Cabin Class, the great doors of Cunard? Perhaps it was my grandmother polishing her brass plaques, light of her skipping sea miles and common sense.

My father had loved Uta. Stella remembered him on the ferry to Staten Island, bringing her a game of iron filings under a sheet of plastic. By using a magnetic pen she could pull the iron chips into patterns and faces. She had drawn a picture of my father and her mother making love in a children's animal park. Papa had seen it and shut himself further away.

I am my father's daughter. I look like him. Stella has her mother's eyes. I do not know what this signifies, if anything at all.

Perhaps some things take more than a single lifetime to complete. Perhaps I too have begun to imagine more than can be seen with the instruments we as yet possess.

'Signs, shadows, wonders.' Abel sat rocking in his chair, listening to our story, rolling the diamond between finger and thumb.

'A dybbuk,' he said.

'Papa,' said Stella.

Abel alternatively shook and nodded his head, and finally he dropped the diamond into Stella's palm.

'It is given to you,' he said.

Walk with me. The streets, the cross-streets, the Hudson river where the cattle used to come up to the abbatoir. Stella, dismantling and rebuilding the invented city, showing me what had been and what had not been, sweat and ingenuity of the slowly hoisted dream.

The difficulty. The dream. To pan the living river that you are and find gold in it. But the river moves on, never step in the same river twice, time surging forward and sometimes leaving a caracol, its half-turn backwards that mocks the clock.

My time, my father's time, my grandmother's time. Now separate, now flowing together, and joined with the floods and cries of men and women I have never met, places and years that snag their movement in mine and choose me, for a moment, as a conscious depot of history.

What is it that you contain? The dead, time, light patterns of millennia opening in your gut. What is salted up in the memory of you? Memory past and memory future. If the universe is movement it will not be in one direction only. We think of our lives as linear but it is the spin of the earth that allows us to observe time.

Walk with me.

Two sparrows were diving at a bread roll. A woman's shoes were spattered with mud. A small child in long socks poked at the bucket of eels outside the Chinese grocery store. His father's belly swagged over his head. Through the window, in the barber's shop, white towels were bibbed around weathered necks. An old man shuffled inside his sandwich board: THE END IS NIGH.

The freight train and the rose garden. The hot-dog stand and the evening news. Closing Down Sale. Everything Must Go.

From a room up above, the smell of frying. Above that, Mozart on a tinkly piano '. . . *Purché porti la gonnella . . .*'

From the open window of an attic a canary cage dangled over the street, its occupant feather and beak in song.

They were raising the roof next door. Girders in the mouths of cranes, the steel squawk of the construction bird, hard-hats crane lit, beams and specks of men balanced on the threshold of the built and the unbuilt.

Up higher, far away, the red digital flash of date and time: November 10 19:47 (Sun in Scorpio. City of New York).

Blue sky light had turned black, red tracks of automobiles wound across the bridge, safety lights on brake reflectors, red on red.

The universe hangs here, in this narrow strait, infinity and compression caught in the hour. Space and time cannot be separated. History and futurity are now. What you remember. What you invent. The universe curving in your gut. Put out your hand. Kiss me. The city is a scintilla, light to light, quartz and neon of the Brooklyn Bridge and the incandescence of the stars.

They were letting off fireworks down at the waterfront, the sky exploding in grenades of colour. Whatever it is that pulls the pin, that hurls you past the boundaries of your own life into a brief and total beauty, even for a moment, it is enough.